Lawfully Witnessed

Brides of Cedar Falls, Book #1

Jo Grafford, writing as Jovie Grace

SECOND EDITION: This book was originally part of the Lawkeeper Series. It has since been rewritten and expanded to launch the **Brides of Cedar Falls Series** — uplifting historical romance full of faith, hope, love, and cowboys!

ISBN: 978-1-63907-067-1

Acknowledgments

Many heartfelt thanks to my editor, Cathleen Weaver, and my awesome beta readers for reading and sharing their thoughts about this story. I also want to give a shout-out to my Cuppa Jo Readers on Facebook for reading and loving my books!

Chapter 1: The Summons

March, 1862

"We're at war, Papa. It's only a matter of time before the fighting reaches Atlanta."

Twenty-year-old Anna Kate cringed at the sound of angry male voices downstairs. The war might as well be taking place in their living room from the number of family arguments it had sparked lately. However, her brothers were right. The Monroe family could not afford to hide their heads in the sand any longer. Trouble was coming their way, whether they were ready or not.

She stood silently in front of the dressing mirror in her second-story bedchamber as she fluffed her long blonde hair enticingly around her shoulders. Staring critically at her pink silk gown with its ruffled chiffon overlay, she wished more than anything there was a party she could wear it to this evening. Like most folks, she agreed the war was a horrible thing and sorely wished it would go away, but that didn't keep her from appreciating how nice the newest batch of soldier recruits looked in their uniforms. It made her heart flutter just thinking about all those royal blue trousers and light gray jackets. The scarlet trim edging them and rows of shiny brass buttons brought to mind no end of breathtaking acts of bravery and heroism.

She indulged in a gusty sigh of self-pity, not wanting to dwell on the battles to come. At the moment, she was wallowing in a different sort of melancholy, because the war had stolen more than her family's peace. It had also utterly destroyed the all-important social season that every southern belle of marriageable age looked forward to.

There would be no parties for her this year — no teas, picnics, musicales, or holiday gatherings. With rumors of military skirmishes popping up all over the state of Georgia, Papa wasn't willing to let her out of his sight these days. He wouldn't even let her go on horseback rides or walks any longer. She'd all but become a prisoner in their home. If something didn't change soon, she was going to spiral into utter madness! A girl could only paint so many watercolors or practice so many hours on the pianoforte. She desperately needed something more to do or, better yet, some place else to go.

Lost in contemplation, she nibbled on her lower lip as she glided to her bedchamber door. Turning the knob and pushing it open, she paused when a knock sounded on the front door. *Dear heavens, let it be the milk man. Or a neighbor.* Not someone bearing any more bad news.

She glided from her room to peer over the balcony railing to the grand foyer below. Their butler of many years, Frederick, materialized as silently as a ghost to answer the door. He was an unsmiling, middle-aged man with his hair slicked back by too much pomade. She wrinkled her nose at the somber black suit he persisted in wearing, despite her many attempts over the years to elevate his wardrobe to something less funereal. A pin-striped waistcoat, perhaps, or even a vest. Something with a dash of color, for pity's sake.

After a hushed exchange of words with someone she could not see from her vantage point, she observed him accepting a small white envelope on the silver tray he always carried with him.

He firmly shut the front door, performed a perfect pivot on the heels of his perfectly shined shoes, and squarely met her gaze as if he'd already known she was standing there. Since she was a small child, she'd always wondered if he had eyes in the back of his head, a trait she found most irritating.

"It is a letter, Miss Anna Kate," he announced in a smooth, well-modulated voice that she sorely doubted even the war could frazzle. "For you."

"For me?" Her flagging spirits perked at the thought of receiving news from out of town. So often these days, the mail was delayed or failed to run at all. "How wonderful!" She moved down the stairs, as fast as a proper lady was allowed, to whisk the precious envelope from his tray.

"Ahem," he said quietly as she wordlessly spun away from him.

"Thank you, Frederick." Knowing the man was as curious as she was about the letter, though far too hoity-toity to ask any questions, it delighted her to no end to dismiss him with a flutter of her fingers. Whoever had written her and whatever news they had to impart was for her eyes alone.

The dinner hour was fast approaching, so she didn't return to her bedchamber. Instead, she slipped inside the front parlor and cozied herself in a windowed alcove. Normally, dinner time was her favorite time of day — the *only* time of day, really, that she could pretend the Monroes were still one big happy family. But her menfolk seemed bent on ruining that little fantasy of hers this evening. She tried to block out their bellowing as she turned the envelope over to see how it was addressed.

Why, it was from Winifred Monroe, her father's only sister! She was an eccentric woman several years his senior, a confirmed spinster who'd thumbed her nose at their southern roots and moved west over a decade earlier.

Aunt Win! Though most of the family considered her an oddball, Anna Kate had always enjoyed her infrequent visits during holidays, funerals, and such. Her Aunt Winifred was an outspoken woman with an infectious laugh, one of those rare creatures who wasn't afraid to speak her mind.

Anna Kate's father's voice rose in agitation from the other end of the hallway, making her pause before opening the letter. "I don't believe in shirking one's duties, son. However, we have a rail and supply center to keep running downtown. I know it may not seem as glorious as shouldering a rifle, but who do you think gets those rifles to where they're going?" He sounded very much the part of Jack Monroe, or Jack Senior as his closest friends and associates liked to call him, the proud owner of a line of bustling shipping yards and warehouses. From what she understood, he more or less cornered the market on storage and shipping in the greater Atlanta area, which served as the nerve center for their region. It meant her family was wealthy — vastly wealthy in ways that even the war itself couldn't diminish. In fact, Monroe Industries had been booming with business ever since the wheels of the war machine started turning.

"Profits, you mean!" her oldest brother, Jackson,

growled. "That's all you've ever cared about, isn't it? The bottom line and nothing else."

Anna Kate rolled her eyes and tried to block out their angry voices. They'd been going at each other's throats like rabid dogs since daybreak. It was the same old argument they'd been having ever since the war began.

Jackson was a Union sympathizer and wanted their family to pack up and flee to their vacation home in the Blue Ridge Mountains, whereas Jack Senior had no intention of abandoning their family business.

"I know it's not as exciting as following the drum, and it may not feel as adventurous as hightailing it to the mountains, son, but this is our home," her father's voice rumbled. "We work and we carry on, the same way as every other Monroe has been doing for generations."

Jackson made a growling sound that traveled menacingly down the hallway and across the parlor to the velvet divan where Anna Kate was perched. "And when the Confederacy finally ratifies that Conscription Bill they've been yammering on and on about? Then what, Papa?" There was a pointed silence, during which she could envision the glare he was giving Jack Senior. "I reckon you'll just quietly keep running our rail and supply business when they come to cart Will, Grady, and myself off to Heaven only knows where?"

Conscription! Allowing the letter to drop unopened into her lap, Anna Kate clapped a hand over her mouth. She couldn't bear the thought of watching Jackson being drafted and taken away from her, much less Will and Grady. Their younger brothers were but teens! Surely, the Confederacy would consider them a mite young for donning a uniform and picking up a rifle.

Snatching up the letter from Aunt Win, she pushed

aside the heavy brocade curtains separating the alcove from the rest of the parlor. "Papa!" she gasped. Throwing all decorum aside, she lifted her skirts and ran down the wide tiled hall. "Papa!" She rounded the corner and skidded to a halt in the arched doorway leading to the library.

Two pairs of eyes stared back, as blue as her own. Jack Senior was standing by the mantle in one of his dark business suits. The evening sunlight pouring through the picture window illuminated the navy wool and silk weave of the fabric and the custom tailored stitches that held it together.

"Well, there's my favorite southern belle." An indulgent smile tugged the corners of her father's mouth, and the tiny lines at the edges of his eyes became more pronounced. "I trust you had an enjoyable afternoon, sugar?"

"Don't, Papa," she choked. Couldn't he see she was in no frame of mind to engage in small talk about her painting and embroidery projects? "I couldn't help overhearing what you said about the Conscription Bill." Her heart pounded with trepidation as she faced her oldest brother, a hand fisting her skirts in agitation. "Is it true, Jackson? Are they truly getting close to passing it?"

He stood across the room from her with his feet firmly planted on the Persian rug beside the pianoforte, arms crossed and jaw clenched in stubbornness. "I believe it is both likely and imminent," he affirmed. The chill in his voice and stance were directed at their father, not her.

"Then what are we going to do?" Her voice dropped to a fearful whisper. They'd lost their mother to a fever a few years earlier. Anna Kate couldn't bear the thought of losing anyone else she loved.

"My concern, exactly!" Jackson declared harshly.

"What are we going to do, Papa? And whatever it is, we'd best do it soon before the choice is taken out of our hands."

Jack Senior grew very still, and his eyes took on an icy cast that Anna Kate had never seen before. "This *is* my choice, son. That's what I've been trying to tell you all along. If you're looking for my blessing to do otherwise, I'll give it and gladly, but this is where I'll be staying."

Dread filled Anna Kate's chest. She was sick of the war and beyond weary of the way it was dividing her beloved family.

Jackson slowly uncurled his arms to fist his hands at his sides. "That's it?" He sounded shocked and incredulous. "You're throwing your support to the plantation owners? Why?" He looked incensed. "Slavery is wrong, Papa, and you know it. You've admitted it in so many words to me, yourself."

His father angrily batted the air with his hand. "Bah! I'll never own a slave, and I've been doing everything in my power to end such a morally repugnant practice for years. But the war is about more than that, son. It's about fighting to defend what's ours. Our families, our homes, our land, and our businesses." His tone grew tighter. "If you've got your stubborn head set on having an answer from me today, then you'll have it, by George! This is where I'm taking my stand yesterday, today, and tomorrow." He pointed to the floor. "Running Monroe Industries is my contribution to the cause of freedom, just like it was my father's contribution and my grandfather's contribution before that."

Anna Kate's agonized gaze met her brother's furious one. No more words were required. After months of Jackson's goading, Papa was finally choosing a side. He'd been born a southern man, and he would die a southern man.

She dropped her head and stared blindly at the letter in her hand as a deathly silence settled around them.

"Is that a letter, sugar?" her father inquired after a pregnant pause.

She nodded mutely, not yet able to meet his gaze. "It is from Aunt Win." She held it out to him without looking up.

"It's addressed to you, sweetheart," he noted in a mild voice. "Why don't you open it and read it to us?" Waving at her to join him, he walked around the velvet sofa, each footstep echoing with dreaded finality against the hardwood floor.

She sat on the cushion beside him and mechanically tore open the envelope. The scent of her aunt's favorite lavender water assailed her nose as she untucked the letter and opened it.

My dearest niece,

I hope this letter finds you in better health than me. Alas, the doctor says my rheumatism is getting worse and has advised me to seek out a companion. My man of business handles most of the day-to-day work for the railroad spur. However, my duties continue to require an overwhelming amount of correspondence. Naturally, with your lovely penmanship, your name was the first that came to mind, sweet girl. I do not know the odds of that doting father of yours being willing to part with you for any length of time, but I'll gladly keep you in Cedar Falls as long as he can spare you. At the very least, it will give you a break from the horrid war...

Anna Kate hastily skimmed the rest of her aunt's letter, right down to the part where she sent her love to them all. "I should go," she announced to no one in particular.

As much as she hated the idea of being away for an extended period from her father and brothers, her aunt was right. She sorely needed a break, but not from the war. She needed a break from the constant duel of words taking place in her own home, and she didn't mind in the least that her visit to Texas would require some industry on her part. Penning letters for her aunt would give her something meaningful to do. Something that mattered.

"I agree, my dear," her father noted in such a gentle voice that it made Anna Kate's eyes sting with tears. She'd expected his vehement opposition to the idea.

"You're sending me away," she muttered, blinking rapidly to hold the sting of moisture in her eyes at bay.

"That I am," he sighed, moving off the couch to crouch down in front of her. "Jackson has the right of it, love. I should have sent you to a safer place months ago." He reached for her hand and cradled it between his two strong, sturdy ones. "I've been selfish in keeping you here like a caged animal. You were meant to fly free, little bird." He squeezed her hand.

She shook her head fiercely. She might not always agree with his decisions, but selfishness was not what motivated him. It was love. "No, Papa, I—"

"Let me finish," he begged in a voice rough with emotion. "I cannot stomach the thought of parting with you, Will, and Grady, but that is exactly what I must do. It is the only way I can ensure you will remain safe, considering what is coming." He drew an uneven breath.

The stinging behind her eyelids grew worse. "But Papa—"

"No buts, sugar. I promised your mama this was exactly what I would do when the time came."

She tasted bitterness. He was referring to the war again,

always the dratted war! "And Jackson?" The first tear escaped and slid down her cheek as she whipped her head up to meet her brother's troubled gaze. He was more opposed to the war than anyone she knew, yet she could already read his decision. It was written across his features and mirrored in his clear blue eyes. He did not intend to accompany her and their younger brothers to Texas.

He nodded to affirm her fear. "I'll stay with Papa."

"Oh, Jackson!" She didn't know what else to say.

"My place is with him, Anna Kate. War or no war, I'll not be leaving him alone."

She stood, sobbing silently at the finality in his voice. When Jackson got like this, she knew there was no changing his mind. He could be as stubborn as Papa sometimes.

"I'll stay, too," she choked. Her earlier woes about the lack of parties in town seemed awfully petty now. There were far bigger things at stake. If Jackson could sacrifice the things he'd rather be doing, then so could she.

"No, sugar. You will not." Papa rose to stand before her. "Jackson is right. You and your younger brothers need to head to safer ground." When he gathered her in his arms, she knew with sudden certainty that one rift in their family had been mended at long last. The war around them was erupting to newer, more bitter levels; but there would be no more fighting within the walls of their home. The Monroes were united again. It was a pity it had taken a looming and indefinite separation to bring about the peace in their family.

"I'm going to miss you, Papa," she quavered against his shoulder. Her heart ached already.

"Not half as much as I shall miss you," Jack Senior muttered into her hair. "God go with you, my precious girl. Look after your brothers."

"I will, Papa."

"I'll come for the three of you the moment the war is over."

Her shoulders shook as her emotions overtook her. It was a promise they both knew he might not be able to keep. Nevertheless, she would be praying day and night that he would do exactly that.

THE NEXT MORNING, PAPA AND JACKSON RODE WITH Anna Kate, Will, and Grady to the train depot in their family's stately carriage. She tried not to chuckle as her younger brothers groaned and complained about the number of travel bags and trunks their housekeeper, Tanya, had helped her pack. She knew their biggest fear was that they might be stuck helping her lug them the rest of the way. *Mercy me!* Of all the people she was leaving behind, she would sorely miss the maternal, doting attentions of Tanya Cunningham. She was more than hired help. She was a widow who had more or less adopted their family as her own and treated them as such. Anna Kate had made the woman promise at least a dozen times to take care of Papa and Jackson in her absence.

"This is it." Mr. Monroe rapped smartly on the wall of the carriage to indicate where he wanted their driver, Felix, to halt.

Anna Kate had never been fond of goodbyes, but she was especially dreading this one. "Don't say it," she choked as Jackson enveloped her in a gigantic hug. They'd always been close, like two peas in a pod. This was going to be their longest separation to date. "Don't say one blessed thing that will make me cry again, else I'll never forgive you."

"I didn't intend to," he grumbled. "I was only going to urge you to keep your guard up against any and all unscrupulous rogues of the male species in my absence."

"I declare," she teased, her spirits rising several degrees at the underlying affection in his words. "I might actually find a beau if you're not around to threaten bodily harm to every gentleman who dares to look in my direction."

He flicked her nose affectionately. "Just fulfilling my brotherly responsibilities. You're as pretty as a peach, Anna Kate. Everyone east of the Mississippi knows it, and everybody west is about to find out." Though he kept his tone of voice light, he looked genuinely concerned.

She flushed in appreciation. "Says the charming bachelor with the mile-long line of wishful debutantes batting their lashes at you every day of the week."

"Pshaw!" He gave her a look of sheer disgust and rolled his eyes.

"I'm right," she jibed, "which you're making no effort to deny."

"Go, minx." He gave her a playful shove. "Go, before I change my mind and send Frederick with you."

"Heaven forbid!" She did not have to fake the shudder that worked its way through her.

Thanks to Jackson's teasing, Will and Grady's squabbling, and her father becoming distracted by a business associate who was passing by, Anna Kate was able to board the train with dry eyes. Her heart was full of a dozen unspoken fears and worries, though.

She drew a deep breath as she stepped inside the dining car where they would begin their journey. Momentarily closing her eyes to collect her emotions, she promptly bumped into something warm and solid. "Oomph!" Her hands flew out, and her eyelids snapped open. She found herself staring into the amused dark eyes of a handsome, broad-shouldered stranger. His tall frame was folded compactly into a black suit, a gold paisley waistcoat like the kind she'd been trying so hard to get Frederick to wear, and a snowy dress shirt with a bolo. The brim of his Stetson was pulled rakishly low.

Oh, my! Her heartbeat quickened at the realization she'd gone and run into her first honest-to-heavens cowboy before leaving Atlanta. It was both unexpected and a thousand shades of wonderful. Ignoring the vague twinge of concern about why a man his age wasn't wearing a military uniform, she treated him to one of her most ladylike smiles — one that was both gracious and apologetic. She did not wish to appear overeager or starved for company, though she certainly was.

"My apologies, sir." Her voice held a breathless quality that had nothing to do with the jolt of their impact and everything to do with his towering frame and nearness. Their proximity incidentally treated her to a delightful whiff of his aftershave, which further underscored his sheer maleness.

"Pardon me, ma'am." He tipped his hat at her and shot her a lopsided grin that sent a delicious shiver through her midsection. "Pray assure me you're none the worse for our collision."

Mercy, but he was handsome in a tanned, outdoorsy way, though his baritone held a puzzling hint of the north. It wasn't the accent she would have expected of a man returning west. Unless he'd entered the dining car by mistake, however, that was exactly where he was heading.

"I am quite fine, Mr. Ah..." Perhaps it was forward of her, flirtatious even, but Anna Kate was dying to know the man's name and why she'd not previously met him. Her family was acquainted with just about every noteworthy person in Atlanta, so she was certain they'd never before been introduced. Was he merely passing through Atlanta on business? Would they be riding together on the train for long? She suddenly hoped so!

"Gregory Armstrong, ma'am." He held out a large hand.

"Pleased to meet you, Mr. Armstrong." What a gorgeous name! No, she couldn't think of any Armstrongs living in Atlanta. He must be passing through, then. She intended to simply touch her fingers to his, but he enveloped her slender hand with his much larger one and gave it a firm shake.

"I, ah...am Anna Kate Monroe." She deplored the hitch of hesitation in her voice, wondering where her lifetime of southern aplomb had flown to.

"The pleasure is all mine, Miss Monroe." He boldly lifted her fingers to brush his hard mouth lazily across her knuckles.

Good gracious! I beg to differ. She had to dig deep to summon enough poise to quell another shiver of delight. Her sadness at leaving home dimmed considerably beneath the prospect of traveling with such a mysterious and charming stranger, one with an utterly delicious sounding name.

Gregory Armstrong. She repeated his name in her head, hearing the hint of northern starch in it all over again.

Maybe Papa and Jackson were right. Maybe it was time to take a break from the war-riddled south. Though it was a thousand shades of frivolous and silly of her, she was already hoping that the fascinating cowboy who was oh-so-slowly lowering her hand would be around for a decent leg of the journey.

Chapter 2: The Mission

A Union officer with several years of battlefield experience, Captain Gregory Armstrong was trained to keenly observe his surroundings — especially when he was on a top secret assignment like the current one. His ability to rapidly absorb and memorize details had saved the lives of countless soldiers under his command.

This morning, however, it didn't feel one bit like work to study Miss Annabelle Monroe's rapidly changing expressions. If she turned out to be the war criminal his superiors suspected, she was a truly incredible actress. The way her eyes had widened when she'd bumped into him, along with the infusion of rosiness to her high cheekbones, didn't feel feigned.

Her eyes were a striking shade of blue — not half gray or nearly hazel, like so many other people he'd encountered. Instead, they possessed the merest hint of purple, making him think of a field of wild cornflowers. The gown she wore nearly matched her eyes, with yards and yards of silk cascading over an impressive layer of petticoats. The war certainly hadn't been unkind to the Monroe's bank accounts.

"May I escort you to your table, Miss Monroe?" Gregory crooked an arm at Anna Kate and was delighted when she looped her gloved hand through it after only a brief hesitation. The shyness in her touch made him wish he was doing nothing more than escorting a lovely lady down the aisle of the luxury Pullman dining car.

She tipped her face up to his in blushing amusement. "You're about to meet the two fierce watchdogs I am traveling with."

He grinned at her description of her younger brothers, not finding anything about the two fancily dressed gentlemen even remotely fierce. Come to think of it, they weren't all that skilled as watchdogs, either. They'd boarded ahead of her, laughing and jostling each other good-naturedly, and had already claimed a plush upholstered bench in one of the dining booths. Engaged in some sort of brotherly debate, both were nursing silver mugs of whatever beverage they'd ordered. Neither were paying much attention to their sister, which Gregory found more than a little odd. In his experience, war criminals generally weren't so calm and relaxed. Nor so young.

According to Gregory's sources, William Monroe was nineteen, and Grady Monroe was sixteen. He was burning with curiosity to learn what role such junior siblings could possibly be playing in their family's alleged crimes. From his current vantage point, they looked like normal lads in their teens.

Gregory experienced a stab of discomfort at the necessity of viewing them as potential traitors to their nation. Then the moment was gone. Traitors came in every shape and size. Such were the unpleasantries of war.

As a Union officer, he was only doing his job, proudly serving in the capacity of an investigator. Some of his comrades went so far as to call him a spy. It was a title he didn't care for, though he supposed he was a spy of sorts, since he wasn't at liberty to state his true occupation or mission to those he met during his travels. He wasn't ashamed of what he did for a living, though. Men like him were vital to the cause of reuniting a divided nation. He did what he was assigned, going where the job took him and notifying his commander of any intelligence that might be useful in winning the war.

Right this moment, the job was leading him to Cedar Falls, Texas to follow up on a lead that the Monroe family was neck deep in transporting record numbers of fighting men, barrels of ammunition, and other valuable resources from out west to supply the Confederate Army. If the allegations proved true, the rail lines leading from San Antonio to Atlanta would become the Union's next big target for extermination.

William Monroe glanced up to give Gregory a once-over as he and Anna Kate approached. He nodded stiffly while shuffling a deck of cards on the small mahogany table resting between him and his brother. His hair was a few shades darker blonde than his brother's, and his nose was slightly crooked, as if it had been previously broken. Both brothers were sporting natty travel suits, sideburns, and goatees. Again, Gregory was surprised when neither brother exhibited more than a cursory interest in the stranger walking so amicably at the side of their sister.

Gregory tipped his hat at them, anyway.

"These two scamps are my brothers, Will and Grady," Anna Kate trilled, waving a hand in their direction. "Boys, this is Mr. Gregory Armstrong, from, er..." Her voice dwindled as she sent a half-flirtatious, half-inquiring glance in his direction. The movement made her long blonde curls dance around her slender shoulders, while her gaze dueled playfully with his.

An answering chuckle rumbled from deep inside his chest that he felt powerless to hold in. Ah, but Anna Kate was turning out to be a cheeky southern lass! Gone was her earlier blushing uncertainty. In its place was a veneer of gushing politeness. Just beneath the surface, however, he sensed she was as curious as a kitten and as watchful as a hawk — all traits a body might expect in the enterprising young socialite she appeared to be. Or a person who was knowingly and willingly betraying her nation.

Gregory made a mental note to keep up his guard around her at all times, lest he become sucked in by her fatal enchantment.

"I'm from Boston, originally," he supplied smoothly. He'd learned it was best to give truthful answers, or mostly truthful answers, at any rate. It avoided awkward questions down the road when topics such as his accent were brought under scrutiny. "However, I spend a good deal of time on the road these days. I'm an investor with holdings in the Northern Pacific, Union Pacific, and Southern Pacific railroads." He adopted the slower drawl he'd practiced, to exude the air of a gentleman of leisure. "I'm currently exploring options to extend my holdings to the Santa Fe line."

It was sheer fiction, of course. His captain's salary kept food on the table and his trousers mended, but it didn't stretch far enough to build an investment portfolio. Not even close. The only reason he was traveling in a Pullman car with the Monroe siblings was because the Union Army was paying for it.

"How far are you going, sir?" Anna Kate inquired in a burst of unexpected boldness. "As it happens, we're riding all the way to San Antonio to see our aunt. Well, technically, she lives in a much smaller town outside the city. A place called Cedar Falls. I doubt you've heard of it."

Again, he didn't have to pretend. His surprise was genuine. He'd known their destination, but hadn't known they were traveling to visit family. Or so they claimed. It was yet another piece of the massive puzzle he was busy constructing.

"Well, fancy that! I happen to be heading that way myself. To San Antonio, that is." He grinned. "What are the odds?"

Will's gaze flickered across his person once more. "Our father is in the shipping business," he offered in a moderately bored tone. "Perhaps you met him during your stay in town? Jack Monroe of Monroe Industries."

Or Jack Senior, as the shipping icon was more commonly called by his business associates. From what Gregory had gathered so far, Mr. Monroe's Atlanta holdings were sizable — bordering on the monopoly level — and his influence in the region was a force to be reckoned with.

It wasn't immediately apparent if the lad was boasting about his father's importance or slyly conducting an interrogation of his own. Gregory was careful to keep his response nonchalant. "I've certainly heard of him. But, no. I did not have the pleasure of making his acquaintance." He infused a suitable dose of regret into his voice. "Perhaps I will be more lucky on my next pass through Atlanta."

Grady, who'd been silent until now, shot him a boyish grin of offhand acceptance, as if Gregory's fictitious claim to being an investor somehow put them on the same social level. "Would you like us to deal you in, Mr. Armstrong?"

"Certainly, and I prefer to be called Gregory." Knowing a high society man wouldn't wait for more of an invitation, he handed Anna Kate onto the bench beside the lad, claiming the empty spot across from her as if it had been reserved for him. He lounged back against the cushion and winked at her. "I have too many miles ahead of me to stand on ceremony." He was brazenly inviting her to call him by his given name. "Deal me in, lads."

Anna Kate's fair cheeks colored prettily, but she said nothing. Instead, she returned to her feet with a swish of skirts.

Gregory mirrored her movements, arching his eyebrows expectantly at her.

She lifted her chin a notch. "While you gentlemen are counting cards and pretending not to cheat, I think I'll explore the car and find out what they have in the way of refreshments." Twirling around, she glanced coyly over her shoulder a few times as she sauntered away, as if expecting Gregory to follow her.

When he returned to the cushioned bench and proceeded to pick up the cards he'd been dealt, her lush lips settled into a pout. He continued to watch her out of the corner of his eye as she sashayed down the aisle, exploring the car. A few minutes later, she ended up seated on a stool at the far end of their car.

Interesting. Gregory wondered if she was previously acquainted with the trio of businessmen she was chatting with. A tidily dressed woman in spectacles was silently perched next to one of the men. Unlike Anna Kate's lavish gown, her much plainer one had a schoolmarmish look to it. On the bar in front of their group rested a cluster of tall crystal glasses.

Though Gregory was supposed to be gathering intelligence on the Monroe family as a whole, he soon became so engrossed in watching Anna Kate's energetic hand movements and animated expressions, that he missed a cue and lost the round.

Will snorted, casting a knowing glance in his sister's direction. "She's pretty, isn't she?" He gathered their cards from the table to reshuffle them.

"Yes, indeed." *A thousand times, yes!* Though Gregory was surprised by the blunt question, there was no point in dodging it. A wealthy gentleman investor would presume himself eligible for courting such a lovely creature. He would exude a smooth, suave level of confidence. Fortunately, Gregory didn't have to fake the admiration part of his feelings. Though they'd just met, Anna Kate Monroe interested him for reasons he couldn't explain away with gut logic. Beneath her lavish depth of social polish, there was a playful innocence he hadn't expected. A softness. A certain vulnerability. Unless it was all an act, of course.

Regardless, it drew him like a siren. He hoped it wouldn't become a problem in the coming days.

"Jackson calls her as pretty as a peach," Grady chuckled. "Half the rogues in Atlanta fancy themselves in love with her, though most of them wouldn't dare admit it around him."

Ah, so Jackson is the real watchdog in the family. It was odd that Anna Kate was traveling without him. Nonetheless, it was an honorable trait in any older brother, even in a man who might be a traitor. Gregory lowered his voice for his next question. "Is she spoken for?" It was early in the game, but it wouldn't hurt for her younger brothers to get the impression he was throwing his hat in the ring as a potential suitor, giving him all the more reason to shadow them during the journey.

Grady pursed his lips thoughtfully "Not at—"

A nudge from his brother's boot against his shin halted whatever he was about to say.

And so the next older brother assumes the role of watchdog. That was all well and good with Gregory. More than good. He was starting to like the two youngest Monroes. They came across as honorable and decent, albeit a bit on the boyish side. Most importantly, his investigative instincts, which rarely steered him wrong, weren't sending up any warning flags about their behavior. If he had to venture a guess at this juncture, they had little to no involvement whatsoever in their family's war efforts.

Most unfortunately, the assumption left their sister as his top suspect. Someone in the Monroe family or company was serving as a liaison between San Antonio and Atlanta, coordinating the constant shipments of supplies that made their way to the Confederate Army. If it wasn't either of the two lads sitting with him at the table, that someone could easily be her.

He waved away Will's offer to deal him another hand. "Are either of you as dry as I am?" He rose from his seat, waving at their near empty mugs.

Will shook his head. "Truth be told, we're as stuffed as Christmas turkeys, only a few sips away from popping." He added in a mocking tone, "Despite the early hour, Cook insisted on serving us a feast before we left the house."

Must be nice to be waited on hand and foot by servants. Accustomed to fending for himself, Gregory couldn't fathom such a thing. "Well, I'm off to wet my whistle at the other end of the car." Only one of the businessmen remained at the bar with Anna Kate by the time he strode up to them. The other two men and the woman with spectacles had vacated their seats. It was the perfect time to give the lingering fellow a little competition for her attention.

She'd wanted him to follow her to the bar. He'd delayed just long enough to let her know she couldn't lead him around by the nose — hopefully long enough to keep the thrill of the hunt going. They had many miles ahead of them, several days' worth, in fact. There was no need to allow himself to get "caught" by her flirtatious overtures too soon.

He claimed the stool to her right that the other woman had vacated. "Do you recommend whatever is in that lovely glass of yours, Miss Monroe?"

She turned her sparkling gaze to his, and he was once more drawn in by her smile and vivacity. "Were you gone so long that we're back to Mr. and Miss again?"

"Only if you wish, madam," he answered with false humility, assuring her with his eyes that he much preferred the opposite.

She chuckled and flicked one glossy curl over her shoulder.

He wondered if it felt as soft and silky as it looked.

"What I wish is for a refill of this scrumptious raspberry lemonade." She nodded at the attendant behind the counter, who hastened to comply with her request.

"Make that two, sir." Gregory slid a few coins across the tabletop, enough to cover both their drinks.

To his surprise, the beverage turned out to be carbonated.

Anna Kate keenly watched his expression change. "It's imported from London," she explained smugly. "Do you like the bubbles?"

He wrinkled his nose in consideration, eliciting a chuckle from her. "It's my first time trying it," he confessed, both amused and intrigued by the unique sensation rolling and sizzling across his tongue.

He spared an impatient glance at their neighbor, hoping the man would leave once he realized Gregory intended to monopolize Anna Kate's attention. Up close, he determined the businessman was not the competition he'd originally presumed. For one thing, his tie was folded in reverse, as if someone else had done it for him while facing him; and there was a suspicious smudge of what looked to be dried milk or hot cereal on the fabric of his shoulder. It was in the shape of a tiny finger. His guess was the man was not only married, but also the father of at least one small child.

"I am still forming an opinion of it. Perhaps you can help." Gregory casually addressed the gawking man, drawing him into their conversation. "What is your opinion, sir? Is this bubbling concoction something you would order for your wife or your child?"

With a startled mumble that was difficult to understand, the man leaped from his stool and beat a hasty retreat to the center of the car, leaving his beverage unfinished.

"Well!" Anna Kate huffed, staring at the crystal glass he'd abandoned. She returned her gaze to Gregory. "So much for my hopes of acquiring my first traveling beau," she teased. "How in the world did you deduce he was married? A calculated guess?"

"Not at all." He snorted in disgust. "His tie was folded backwards. By his wife, I presume; and there was an oatmeal stain on his jacket right in the spot where a tiny hand might have been flung in a last-minute embrace."

She silently clapped her hands. "Very clever, Mr. ah..."

"Gregory," he supplied quickly.

"Very clever, Gregory." She studied him in fascination. He was utterly enchanted by the way his name was transformed by her soft alto and southern accent. Like music.

"I was under the impression you were an investor," she continued in her lilting tone. "I see now you are much more than that."

Oh? His senses went on high alert. Had he made a verbal misstep? Had he sent her a wrong cue and thereby given something away about his true identity?

"Yes, indeed. I see it now, sir. You are a wizard." She nodded in satisfaction and took another sip from her glass, allowing her eyes to twinkle over the rim at him.

He was so entranced that he found himself wishing they were indeed two strangers who had met on a train — one ravishing southern belle and one hardened northern officer. Better yet, he wished they'd met in a world where that fact wouldn't make one of them a traitor.

Her smiles spilled over him like sunshine, thawing places in his heart he'd thought were long frozen over. After five years in service to his nation, he'd seen things and done things that weren't easily erased. He'd been instrumental in bringing dozens of men to justice; and, more often than not, they'd ended up dangling from the wrong end of a noose because of it. Some nights, that fact wasn't an easy bedfellow to curl up with.

Alas, his lovely travel companion was awaiting his response to her sally, so he had to think quickly in order to concoct something far more frivolous than the truth. "Ah. You've guessed my secret," he drawled, tipping up his glass for a drink. By the time he lowered it, he'd come up with an appropriately teasing response. "Now it is only a matter of deciding which spell to cast on you to ensure you keep my confidences." He raised one long finger, as if inspired by a sudden thought. "Or to make you forget our conversation altogether." He allowed his voice to sink to a lower, more mysterious note.

She pretended to shiver. "Perhaps I don't want to forget," she murmured. The color in her cheeks blossomed to the shade of summer berries, and there was a bemused sparkle to her eyes. She was enjoying herself, a fact that pleased Gregory to no end. The work he did for a living didn't leave much time for courting. None, in fact. It was a relief to discover he was still capable of entertaining a woman in conversation.

"Perhaps I don't want you to, either, Anna Kate."

She caught her breath at his use of her given name. It was the first time he'd said it aloud, though he'd repeated it a few dozen times inside his head already.

He was more entranced than ever. Was it possible the well-practiced debutante sitting beside him was a wee bit rattled by his presence? It was clear to him she was accustomed to playing parlor games and carrying on light flirtations. It was equally clear to him that she was not as immune to him as she'd originally pretended to be. Normally, the observation would have given him immense satisfaction in knowing he was playing his current role in a convincing manner. Instead, it left him longing to know for certain that Anna Kate Monroe's interest in him was real.

He'd only made her acquaintance minutes earlier, but already he was longing for what was happening between them to be real — every teasing word, every coy glance, every smile. It was an impossible wish, of course. Southern belles didn't court northern spies, especially one who was investigating her family for alleged war crimes. If she ever found out his true mission, at best she would feel betrayed, and rightfully so.

At worst, she would despise him.

Chapter 3: Rail & Supply Intrigue

Gregory traveled two more days without witnessing anything overly suspicious about the three Monroe siblings. By the third morning, he was beginning to wonder if his superiors had made a mistake in sending him to investigate their family. What if the lead he'd been given was wrong? Such things didn't happen often, but they did happen. On one hand, he hoped his sources were incorrect so he could clear the Monroe family name. On the other hand, he hoped he didn't succeed in accomplishing that task too soon. He was in no hurry to claim a business emergency, exit at the next train stop, and cease his role as their travel companion.

"I wish I could sprout wings and fly the rest of the way," Grady grumbled. Hands stuffed in the pockets of his trousers, he was stooped over to peer through the wide panes of glass separating them from the terrain flying past them on the other side. There wasn't much to see during the last hour or so, other than marshes for miles upon endless miles. As they chugged through the lower part of Mississippi, it was clear that the youngest Monroe was suffering from cabin fever.

"Would you care to join me for my morning calisthenics?" Gregory had been in his fair share of foxholes with younger soldiers. He understood the lad had a fountain of restless energy to burn off. Another day of inactivity would only make it worse.

Grady blew out a frustrated breath and spun to face him. "What sort of calisthenics?" he groused.

Gregory knew what that meant. Sure, Grady was bored, but the youthful side of him wanted to first ensure that whatever Gregory was suggesting wouldn't entail too much work. He resisted the urge to laugh. "How about you change into something more..." He waved at the lad's expensive suit and leather shoes. "Well, something more suitable for an athletic event." Hopefully, the teen had brought a riding outfit with him or hunting clothes. Just about any change of clothing would be more appropriate than what he was currently wearing.

Grady's expression brightened. "Gladly, sir. Anna Kate is the one who insisted we stay all trussed up in these blasted travel suits." He tugged at his bolo. "I'm about ready to suffocate in this thing."

Gregory guffawed at the lad's frankness. "I can well understand the feeling." Some of his military uniforms were every bit as insufferable. "Perhaps you could seek out Will and ask if he wants to join us? I'll be waiting for you seven cars down at the gymnasium."

"Seven cars!" Grady exploded. "How in tarnation did you—" He broke off his rant to shake his head. "A gymnasium on a train, eh?" He gave a low whistle. "By all that is holy! Now I've heard of everything."

THE GYMNASIUM CAR WAS A NEW EXPERIMENT, OF sorts, something the train company wasn't advertising widely to its patrons for safety reasons. So far, the space had been used by a troupe of traveling circus performers as well as a handful of athletes. Gregory had stumbled upon its existence quite by accident but had managed to wrangle permission to use it for no additional charge.

There were no porters or attendants present, since the car was simply being transported for delivery across the country to another rail line.

He had his shirt sleeves rolled up and was lifting a twenty pound dumbbell in each hand when the Monroe brothers arrived.

"This is unbelievable," Will breathed, stepping into the car and gazing around the space with wonder. He gave a tentative tug on one of the pulley machines.

Grady gave a whoop of delight and took a running leap to hang from a pair of rings suspended from the ceiling. He hung there, swinging back and forth.

Gregory chuckled and set down his dumbbells. He strode across the car to stand beside the lad. "Pull yourself up again," he urged.

The wiry teen had no difficulty bringing his chin level with his hands, which remained clenched around the rings.

"Now lower yourself until your arms are straight and do it again." Gregory nodded encouragement, while Grady repeated the exercise several more times without too much difficulty.

On his eleventh try, however, his arms began to shake. Regardless, he managed to crank out another three pull-ups before his fingers slid from the rings. With an oomph of exertion, he landed on the balls of his feet and proceeded to rub the numbness from his arms. "Ow!" He gazed up at the rings with new respect. "Who would ever think two silly metal rings could cause so much discomfort?"

Gregory nodded, not having the heart to inform him how sore his muscles would be tomorrow.

"Here. Let me have a go at it." Will shoved his brother none too gently out of the way and jumped up to hang from the rings. He raised and lowered himself in much quicker succession than his brother and managed to crank out seventeen of the exercises in a matter of seconds. The moment his arms started to shake, however, he hopped down and dusted his hands. "That is how it's done, brother."

"You could have done more," Gregory admonished, surprised at how quickly the lad had given up.

"I could." Will gave a decided nod. "But I see no reason to reduce my arms to limp noodles."

"You should always push yourself to your limit." It was natural for Gregory to fall back into the role of a coach and mentor. "It is the only way to get stronger."

"If you say so, old man." Will rolled his eyes. "Why? Do you think you can do more than me?"

For an answer, Gregory launched himself onto the rings. "I do not think I can do more. I know it." Holding the cocky nineteen-year-old's gaze steadily, he cranked out twenty of the exercises without so much as panting.

Grady gleefully took over the counting from there. "Twenty-one. Twenty-two."

It wasn't until Gregory reached thirty that his arms started to ache from the exertion. He managed to crank out five more before having to take his first rest in the hanging position. Then he grunted and sweated his way through yet another five, giving the exercise everything he had in him. War had taught him to take every training opportunity seriously.

Alas, he only made it halfway up the thirty-first pull-up before his arms gave out.

When his feet touched the floor, it took a full minute for the blood to resume circulating properly through his forearms and upper arms. He rolled his shoulders a few times and shook off the twinges of pain. "That is how it's done, Will. And the next time I try this exercise, I'll eke out one more. See if I don't."

Will had the grace to look a tad shamefaced. "So what you're saying is, I need to work until my body shakes like a volcano and protests like a screeching fish wife."

"Yes." Gregory grinned at the teen's colorful description. "Every time."

"Alright, old man. You've made your point." Will sent a playful punch to Gregory's sore bicep, making him grit his teeth to hide a wince. "So, what's next?"

What was next was all the stretching and calisthenics Gregory had originally planned to start them off with. By the time they completed a full hour of exercising, all three of them were drenched with sweat and panting. There was no hiding the light of satisfaction in the eyes of both Monroe brothers, though. They understood they'd just spent an hour doing something more worthwhile than playing another few hands of cards.

Grady laid back on the floor and tucked his hands behind his head. "I reckon we're going to be sore tomorrow, huh?"

You guessed it, champ. Gregory grimaced as he nodded. "For a few days. Your body is young and strong, though. It will soon grow accustomed to a strenuous exercise regimen if you keep at it. Consistency is key." He shot a grin in Will's direction, pleased to note he looked as tired as the rest of them. After Gregory's first admonition, Will had pushed himself even harder than his younger brother. "Since the topic of my age keeps coming up, I am five and twenty. Not as old as you seem to think I am. Just wiser and stronger," he finished in a teasing voice.

"We yield to your superior strength," Will returned sarcastically, "for now. But you'd best watch yourself during our next run at the rings." He eyed the metallic loops hanging from the ceiling. "I'm going to work hard, and I am going to beat you if it's the last thing I do."

Gregory grinned at the challenge, impressed by the determination in Will's voice. "A challenge I am happy to accept." He hoped the lad succeeded. He truly did.

They ended their session and made their way to their private quarters to bathe and change. Gregory was more grateful than ever that he was housed in a luxurious Pullman car for the duration of the trip. He'd never before had access to a bed with such a thick mattress or such soft linens, much less a wash basin or a tub on a train. In the past, he'd ridden in a crowded public car with no place to properly stretch out at night.

Nor had he ever before enjoyed the pleasure of dining in a private cushioned booth where Anna Kate would be waiting for them to break their fast.

———

She eyed them with no small amount of suspicion when the three of them joined her. "What have you been up to?" She reached up to tweak an errant lock of Grady's hair into place.

Their hair was still damp from their baths, and each of them had on a fresh change of clothing. "If we weren't confined to a train," she continued, "I'd venture to guess you'd gone cliff diving or swimming in a lake."

"Nothing so exciting," Grady assured, though the light in his blue eyes and animation in his angular features said otherwise. "Gregory was just showing off in the gym and taunting us to keep up with him."

"I see." Anna Kate's tone indicated she did *not* see, and she continued to cast curious glances at the three of them. There was a softness in her features, however, as her gaze met Gregory's.

His gut told him she approved of the time he was spending with her brothers, which made his chest swell with an unexpected sense of pride. He'd lost his parents at a young age and had been raised by an aging uncle. He'd not known the joy of having a single sibling with whom to spar and goad. Thus, he was very much enjoying the pseudo-sense of belonging it gave him to travel with the Monroes. Plus, he liked Will and Grady — way more than he should have for a man who was supposed to be investigating their family.

The train gave a few warning toots and began to reduce its speed as they approached the next train station. It appeared they would arrive before they finished eating the meal that an attendant was in the middle of bustling to their table.

The three gentlemen dove into their meal with gusto, while Anna Kate picked her fork idly at her potato casserole and omelet. After a few tiny bites, she pushed away her plate. "Unlike the rest of you, I've not had the pleasure of spending an hour in a gymnasium car this morning. Therefore, I am going to step off the train at this next stop to stretch my legs."

Gregory's senses went on full alert. Of all the stops they'd made so far, this would be the first time any of the Monroes had gotten off the train. Why this stop? Why now? They were coasting into Port Gibson, a coastal city in Mississippi. Was it significant or happenstance that it happened to be a key shipping port in the south?

"I am happy to accompany you." He pushed away his plate, though he wasn't finished eating.

She gave a tinkling laugh. "I'm not certain an escort will be necessary. I wasn't planning on venturing any farther than the platform."

He arched a single eyebrow at her, trying to figure out if this was simply more of her sassy repartee or if she truly did not wish him to accompany her. "We're at war, Anna Kate. These are uncertain times. I'd feel better if you'd at least take one of your brothers along."

He knew he had no right to make such a demand. However, he saw no reason to hide the fact that he was truly concerned about her safety.

The color in her cheeks deepened as she stood. "I'll consider it *after* I freshen up and retrieve my cloak. The wind has been rocking our car for the past hour. I imagine it's chilly out." With one last laughing glance over her shoulder at the menfolk in their party, she spun away from the table.

"Will?" A sense of foreboding settled in Gregory's gut as he glanced out the window. The train was swiftly reducing speed as it rolled into the crowded port city. They were going slow enough now for him to make out clusters of soldiers in Confederate uniforms strolling the wharves and milling on the walkways alongside the streets.

"Never fear. I'll go with her, Papa Gregory." Her brother tossed his linen napkin on the table, pushed back his chair, and stretched lazily. "Perhaps I can work some of the soreness out while I'm at it. What say you, Grady? Want to trot along with us?"

"Not a chance." Grady made no effort to hide his shudder as the train squealed its way through a lengthy halt. He waited until the car stopped moving before continuing, "I have no desire to go window shopping for dresses or other feminine gewgaws." Like his brother, he stood and stretched. "I'd much rather find a sunbeam to nap away the morning while everyone else scurries like rats around the city. There will be plenty enough time for exploring when we reach San Antonio."

While the brothers traded their usual light bickers and banter, Gregory jolted in alarm. The willowy frame and mauve silk skirts of the woman hurrying across the train platform were unmistakable. "Your sister," he groaned, pointing at Anna Kate. "She's already left the train."

Instead of looking alarmed, Will merely yawned and returned to his seat. "I figured she'd pull a stunt like that. Not to worry, my friend." He patted the table, as if encouraging Gregory to forget his worries and do the same. "It's Anna Kate we're talking about. Don't let her southern belle looks deceive you. She was raised by Papa and Jackson. That means she carries a pistol in her reticule and can take care of herself."

"Surely you jest," Gregory growled, leaping to his feet to start the painstaking process of elbowing his way to the exit. "Armed or not, she's a lovely lady strolling alone amidst strangers in a port city." He couldn't believe the cavalier attitude of her younger brothers. A harried glance over his shoulder revealed Grady had already disappeared —

presumably to search out the sunbeam he'd mentioned earlier.

His suspicions about the Monroes were instantly rekindled. Had the three of them worked in tandem to distract him, so they could go about their family's war efforts in Port Gibson? According to his conversation with a porter a day ago, cargo was both loaded and unloaded at this stop. As a result, it was going to be one of their longer stops. Approximately two hours if the crew stuck to their planned schedule.

Yanking on his coat and Stetson as he walked, Gregory stepped off the train and headed in the direction Anna Kate had taken. He had to step sideways and make apologies to several other passengers as he jostled his way to the base of the platform stairs. A quick glance in either direction revealed no sign of Anna Kate. His beautiful target had vanished.

Hurrying up to the nearest hackney at the curb, he shouted to the driver, "Which way are the warehouses?"

The fellow looked surprised but jerked his thumb to the left.

"And the dress shops?"

The fellow frowned and straightened his slouched leather hat before twisting his thumb in the other direction. "Jes' a quick stroll down Main Street, mister, if yer lookin' for some ruffles and frills," he smirked and waggled his eyebrows suggestively, "though you don't have to leave the wharves for that, if you know what I mean."

Irritated by the man's lewd suggestion, Gregory nodded his thanks for the information and took off at a jog in the direction of the wharves — not, of course, to seek out the company of any other female besides Anna Kate Monroe.

"Dear God, help me find her," he muttered beneath his

breath. Traitor to her country or not, she was a vulnerable young woman. How dare her brothers let her wander off alone in a crowded port infested with soldiers! He found no comfort in the number of Confederate soldiers roaming the streets. Just because a fellow was wearing a uniform didn't make him a gentleman. He'd seen some of the young recruits back home behave like veritable rogues when left to their own devices.

As Gregory drew within sight of the warehouses, he slowed his pace to take a closer look at the passers-by. There were far fewer women strolling through this part of town, and none of them appeared to be of the reputable sort.

One simpered at him and called, "You lookin' for some company, mister?" Her parted lips revealed a mouthful of rotten teeth.

He hurried past her without comment. "Anna Kate!" he shouted, feeling suddenly desperate. "Where are you?"

"Over here." Her answer came so quickly that he had to wonder if he'd imagined it.

He stomped past another gangway. "Anna Kate!" he shouted again.

"Over here," she repeated more loudly.

He spun in the direction of her voice and found her on the next gangway leading out to a ship. She was holding two salty looking sailors at gunpoint.

He dashed down the gangway, whipping out a pair of six-shooters as he drew abreast of the trio. "What is the meaning of this?"

"Whoa there, guv'nor!" The nearest sailor, who already had his hands raised, pushed them higher in the air. "As you can see, we are unarmed. The little miss with the pistol is the one you should be a'feared of."

"What have these men done to you?" Gregory snarled

at her. "Are you injured?"

"Injured!" the second sailor exploded. "Listen, mister, as my mate said—"

"I did not ask you." Gregory pistol-waved the man into silence. "Anna Kate?" He searched her expression for answers. *What are you doing out here, minx?* He hated thinking the worst of her, but her actions this morning weren't inspiring much trust.

Her lips thinned in irritation. "This man sought me out at the train station, claiming he had a letter for me to deliver to my Aunt Winifred. How in tarnation he knew my name..." She shook her head. "When he led me to the wharves and was joined by his friend, I knew I'd been a fool to trust him." She tightened her grip on her weapon. "I was about to put a hole in each of them and dump them in the ocean. What say you, Mr. Armstrong?"

Both men started babbling at the same time.

"Silence!" Gregory growled. When they fell silent, he demanded in a cold, clipped voice, "How do you know Winifred Monroe? What do you wish to communicate with her?"

The nearest sailor opened and closed his mouth a few times, bringing to mind a gulping fish. "This is her shipping line," he babbled nervously. "Everyone knows that."

"I didn't," Anna Kate interjected sharply. "Now, where is the letter you were crowing so much about?"

"In my pocket," the second man admitted sheepishly.

"Hand it over. Now!" Gregory cocked his pistol and aimed it directly at the heart of his companion. "One wrong move, and I'll blow your friend to Kingdom Come."

"Good gravy guv'nor! It's right here. No lie!" The man who claimed to be in possession of the letter slowly reached inside the pocket of his trousers.

For a split second, Gregory feared the fellow was diving for a weapon, but he merely pulled out the promised white envelope. "Our directions were for you to give it to her unopened." He stressed the last word with a note of warning.

"Me specifically? Why me?" she demanded. "You've yet to explain how you recognized me and knew my name. Or how you knew I would be making this stop, for that matter."

"Yer on the manifest, for Pete's sake," the man muttered, looking down at his feet while he extended the letter to her.

Anna Kate snatched it from him and stuffed it inside her reticule. "Why you went to so much trouble to scare the wits out of me for a simple letter delivery is unpardonable. Go! I don't want to lay eyes on either of you again!" She waved her pistol at them to get them moving.

They took off for their ship as fast as two snakes slithering away in the sand.

"Thank you, Gregory," Anna Kate said softy. "Thank you for coming after me."

"You should not have gone off alone like that." He was so incensed that his voice shook.

"You are right." She clutched her pistol and her reticule tighter. Though her voice was calm, her hands were shaking. "I was foolish enough to think I would be safe on Main Street near the train station. I never dreamt someone would sidle up to me, claiming to be in possession of a message for my aunt."

"And?" Gregory prodded when she fell silent. He firmly grasped her elbow as he steered her back towards Main Street. He wanted so badly to believe her, but the scenario made her look more suspicious than ever.

"My aunt has some explaining to do when we arrive at

Cedar Falls," she declared darkly. "I do not know what she's gotten herself caught up in, but it's no wonder Papa sent me this way to serve as her personal secretary. Clearly, she needs assistance if she's gone and gotten herself mixed up with the likes of those ruffians."

"Her secretary?" He wrinkled his brow at her. "I thought you said you and your brothers were visiting."

"We are, in a manner of speaking." Anna Kate sounded suddenly weary. "To be more precise, we're visiting until the end of the war. Papa said he promised Mama on her deathbed that he would send us to safety before the fighting reached Atlanta, and he means to keep us there until the war ends."

"I see." It was a plausible explanation, one that Gregory desperately wanted to be true. "I hope, for your sakes, your aunt is not involved in anything that would bring harm your way. What do you think is in the letter?"

"Oh, for pity's sake! I don't have the slightest idea, and I'm not certain I have any wish to find out!" Anna Kate snapped. "I want nothing to do with the rogues we just rid ourselves of. Heaven knows I have enough of my own troubles to worry about."

Gregory wanted to believe her. He wanted to so badly his chest ached, but he also knew Anna Kate could be playing a part just like he was. The fact remained that she'd traveled alone to a dangerous part of town and risked her lovely neck to retrieve a simple letter. Unless everything she said was true, and she'd been accosted by a complete stranger for a perfectly random reason, her behavior this morning had not been that of a high society debutante. It was the behavior of a woman who had something to hide.

Chapter 4: Dinner Party

April, 1862

On the first day of April, Anna Kate and her brothers arrived in San Antonio. Their Aunt Winifred was waiting for them at the bottom of the train station stairs beside her driver and gilded carriage.

She was a decade older than their father and a confirmed spinster. She wore a high-necked brown dress, a severely pulled back hair style, and no-nonsense reading glasses.

"Oh, my loves!" Her expression softened several degrees at the sight of them. Though her gnarled limbs were tucked into a wheelchair, she threw her arms open and beckoned them forward. "There are no words to express how good it is to see you again. When I heard all three of you were coming..." she sighed, leaving the rest of her sentence hanging in the air.

"Aunt Win!" Galloping his nearly six-foot frame down the stairs, Will was the first to reach her side.

"My, how you've grown Will!" She ushered him closer so she could gather him in her embrace.

Anna Kate followed her brother at a slower, more sedate pace. Grady remained glued to her side.

Their Aunt Winifred gave a start when she peeked at Grady over her spectacles. "Say it isn't so!" she gasped. "This tall chap is Grady?" She pointed at him while glancing laughingly over at Anna Kate. "He's grown at least a foot since I last saw him. Maybe two."

Anna Kate smiled at the way their aunt's words made his whole face light up. She knew he secretly aspired to be taller than both Jackson and Will.

At last it was her turn to be enveloped in their aunt's lavender-scented embrace.

"I am so glad you've come, child," her aunt murmured against her cheek. "You've no idea how sorely I need your assistance."

Anna Kate squeezed the woman's too-thin shoulders in a gentle hug. "I was sorry to hear your rheumatism has taken a turn for the worse, ma'am."

"Bah!" her aunt spat. She held her niece at arm's length. "It's one of the trials of growing older, love. But just because my health forced me to send for you doesn't mean I intend to waste time blubbering about it now that you're here. Like your father, I have a shipping and rail center to run. That's what occupies most of my days." She gave a decided nod.

Unbelievable! She was truly an incredible human being to remain involved in so much industry, while bound to a wheelchair. "Well, I am here and ready to help." Anna Kate straightened and peeped over her shoulder, hoping to catch sight of Gregory before they departed for her aunt's ranch home in Cedar Falls. She'd only traveled west one other time, back when her mother was alive, but she could still recall how large and spacious her aunt's home was. Then again, that was how a person might describe all of Texas — large and spacious.

Aunt Winifred's shrewd gaze followed hers. "Never you mind about your extra pieces of luggage, dear. This happens to be one of my rail lines. I made sure they knew to deliver your belongings all the way to my doorstep. Come now. We are ready to depart, Rupert." She waved at her driver who promptly opened her carriage door.

"I, ah..." Anna Kate's head swiveled in both directions. She'd promised Gregory an introduction to her aunt if he met them at the curb. It was the least she could do for a potential investor who'd been so kind to her and her brothers throughout their trip.

"Well, what is it, child?" her aunt inquired, eyeing her with thinly concealed impatience.

Grady snorted. "Anna Kate met a handsome fellow on the trip here. I don't believe she's overly anxious to bid him farewell."

"Grady Tyrel Monroe!" Anna Kate exclaimed. "What a thing to say! Why, you and Will visited with him more than I did, between all your sessions in the gymnasium car and your many rounds of cards."

"I wasn't aware you were counting the hours or the minutes where said gentleman spent his time." Grady steepled his fingers beneath his chin and treated her to a devilish grin.

"Oh, for heaven's sake!" She rolled her eyes and turned her back on him, which brought her face-to-face with none other than Gregory Armstrong. "Oh!" She pressed a hand to her chest. "There you are."

His dark eyes searched her face, while his lips turned

upward in one of those half smiles she was coming to adore so much.

"She was looking for you." Grady explained in a loud whisper.

Anna Kate briefly closed her eyes, resisting the urge to fly at him and throttle him right there in the middle of the train station.

"Well, now. Who is this?" her aunt's voice rang out in a cheery welcome.

Anna Kate opened her eyes and drew a long-suffering breath before turning around. "Aunt Win, this is Mr. Gregory Armstrong, a potential investor in the Santa Fe line. We made his acquaintance on our way here. Gregory, this is my dear Aunt Winifred Monroe, who owns and operates one of the shipping and rail centers in San Antonio." A highly profitable one, not that she cared to brag.

"It's a pleasure to meet you, ma'am." Gregory's long legs ate up the distance between them. He bent to take her aunt's hand in his and raised it to his lips.

"I am charmed," the spinster murmured.

Unless Anna Kate imagined it, her aunt's cheeks deepened with color beneath Gregory's lordly treatment.

"Perhaps I could treat you to a cup of coffee or a dinner before my trip to San Antonio is concluded?" He arched a brow at her.

"That sounds lovely." Aunt Winifred raised and lowered her delicate shoulders. "I don't make it to San Antonio very often these days, but I happen to have another trip planned for next week."

"Then it's settled. We shall dine together, madam," Gregory affirmed with a grand sweep of his arms. "I wouldn't mind hearing your thoughts about railroad investments in the region." His expression turned grave. "Pray pardon me bringing up such a dismal topic, but the war is changing things, particularly in the rail industry."

Aunt Winifred's blue gaze snapped with energy behind the lenses of her spectacles. "It is, indeed, Mr. Armstrong. I am pleased to meet another person who understands that. Most of the young bucks who approach me about investing, want to talk about nothing more than how many barrels of wine it takes the quench the thirst in Vicksburg."

Vicksburg wasn't too many miles from the port where Anna Kate held the two sailors at gunpoint. She knew from Gregory's probing gaze that he was remembering the same incident.

"It takes a great many barrels, from what I understand, ma'am." His gaze returned to Annabelle.

"That is does." Aunt Win gave a delighted cackle. "Something just occurred to me, Mr. Armstrong. Something that would be far more delightful than a boring old luncheon where we talk nothing but business. I'd like for you to attend the dinner party I'm giving on Friday. Mind you, there will be music and dancing to offset my invest-ment advice, so you'd best dust off your waltzing shoes."

"It would be my pleasure to attend, ma'am. I thank you for the invitation." Gregory gave her a courtly bow, then turned to Anna Kate to repeat the gesture. "Perhaps you might save a dance for me, Miss Monroe?"

She wrinkled her nose at him. "I'll give it some consid-eration, sir." She teasingly fluttered her lashes at him. "I'm sure you're aware how quickly a dance card can fill."

"Not to worry." He winked at her. "I can always cut in."

Her heartbeat sped at the wicked promise in his gaze.

"Until Friday then, Anna Kate," he said softly, touching his fingers to hers. He inclined his head at her aunt once again. "Ms. Monroe, it was good to meet you, and I thank you again for inviting me to your dinner party." He nodded at her brothers. "Will and Grady, it's been a pleasure traveling together. I hope you will continue the exercise routine I showed you."

"We will!" they chorused.

"Good day to all of you."

"Farewell, Gregory," Anna Kate whispered as his tall shoulders retreated in the crowd. Since their journey west was ended, she would be seeing a lot less of him in the coming days. The thought brought on a wave of melancholy. Her only solace was that he'd promised to attend her aunt's dinner party.

"Well, then." Aunt Win clapped her hands smartly as she shot her niece a curious look. Rupert hastened to swing her carriage door wide. "In you go, loves," she waved them ahead of her, "and we'll be on our way."

AUNT WIN'S RAMBLING RANCH WAS EVEN BIGGER THAN Anna Kate remembered — practically lost in the forest of cedar trees the town was so famous for. A wide veranda spanned the white adobe front of her home, and dormer windows with balconies graced the second story. A lengthy addition on each side of the house turned the structure into a giant U shape.

"Welcome to the Bent Horseshoe Ranch," she declared as her carriage rolled to a stop on the wide, front circle drive.

Anna Kate stared out the window, her mouth agape. "It's different, isn't it, Aunt Win? Bigger. You added on to it."

Her aunt gave a dry chuckle. "Added on, raised the roof,

and extended my property both east and west when the land went up for sale."

"Unbelievable!" Though Anna Kate was impressed, she couldn't help wondering why an unattached spinster wanted to own so much property. "You've done a lot, ma'am."

"For good reason." Her aunt waved at the distant plateaus and mesas. "I couldn't bear the thought of just any ol' wet-behind-the-ears rancher moving in next door and building something to block my view of the mountains." She pursed her lips. "I fully intend to spend the rest of my days enjoying this view."

Anna Kate glanced around in bemusement, knowing her aunt's view of the mountains was from between the limbs of all the cedars surrounding her home. It was still a lovely view. She couldn't wait to pay a visit to the mountains, where the town's other famous attraction rested — the gush of water plunging into the spring below it.

As promised, a crew arrived from the train station within the hour, bearing the rest of Anna Kate's travel bags and trunks. Though Will and Grady hadn't packed nearly as much clothing as their sister, they had a trunk apiece delivered, as well.

"My housekeeper will get you boys settled upstairs," Aunt Winifred announced with a gracious wave of her hand. "You're welcome to share a room or each take a room of your own, whatever you prefer. Nell has aired out the spare bedchambers and freshened up the linens for everyone." She continued to make pronouncements and give orders like a queen the entire time Rupert was wheeling her up the wooden ramp to her front door. "Anna Kate, you may follow me." She beckoned imperiously with one heavily be-ringed hand. "Since we'll be working so closely together, I thought it would be best to have you stay down the hall from me on the main level."

"That sounds wonderful, ma'am." Anna Kate discovered she no longer needed her cloak the moment she stepped inside her aunt's palatial home. That was the only way to describe it. She stared at the massive two-story stone fireplace filling the great room with toasty heat. Despite the brisk morning breezes swirling on the other side of the door, it was a little too warm indoors for her tastes.

There were towering bookcases and plush upholstered furniture with thick claw feet. Not one, but two, pianofortes faced each other on the far side of the room. Why, the place had enough seating to host an honest-to-heavens musicale!

Anna Kate felt like skipping as she followed her aunt down a dimly lit hallway to the rear of the house. It looked as if her nearly dead social agenda was about to revive in leaps and bounds. Friday's dinner party and dance were only the beginning. She could already envision hosting concerts, charades, teas, luncheons, and any number of other get-togethers right here in her aunt's home. Perhaps Gregory Armstrong could extend his stay in San Antonio and attend every one of the events swimming through her mind.

Rupert opened a tall, cherry wood door and ushered them inside.

"For me?" Anna Kate took one look at the four-poster bed drenched in white lace and did a happy twirl in the middle of the room. The space was fit for a princess. There was an ornately carved writing desk just inside the door with a cushioned stool pushed up to it. A nearby sitting area was furnished with a chaise lounge in white velvet. Against the far wall were three oversized armoires, a delicate looking crystal basin, and two wide picture windows overlooking the rear courtyard.

"Of course, it's for you, my dear. Your mother, may she rest in peace, warned me years ago about your extensive wardrobe. I figured your collection would have only grown since then, so I had Rupert move a third armoire into the room, just to be safe."

"You are too kind," Anna Kate breathed, taking another twirl on the Persian rug. "I truly hope you do not intend for me to return south very soon." Though her voice was teasing, she was at least half serious.

"I don't, actually."

Her aunt's blunt response made Anna Kate stop in mid-twirl. "Oh?" She didn't mind the thought of a prolonged stay, but her aunt's tone indicated she had more to say on the topic.

"Your father wrote and asked if I'd keep you and your brothers until the war is over."

Anna Kate's excitement faded. The war rose like a tall dark specter inside her head, casting its shadow over everybody and everything in her life. And there was no end in sight to it. Unless the good Lord intervened, there was no telling how many years it could stretch on.

"It's safer here, love," her aunt pointed out quietly. "Farther from the fighting."

"True." Anna Kate winced at the reminder that her father and oldest brother were very much still in danger. "Do you think it will ever end, Aunt Win?" She hated how small her voice sounded.

"I do, sweetheart. Not soon enough for my tastes, but it will end. Eventually. In the meantime," she continued in a brisker tone, "there's a rail line I need your help running. If it makes you feel any better, you'll be helping your father and the entire south in the process of keeping it chugging along."

"What do you mean?" Anna Kate had been under the impression that she was being sent west to get away from the war, not to become embroiled in it all over again from this many miles away.

"As if you didn't already know!" Her aunt shot her an incredulous look. "Surely your pa has told you that the war won't be won on the backs of young soldiers alone, dear. It takes railroad tracks, roads, and bridges to get the supplies that feed the war machine from one end of the country to the other."

"I reckon that makes sense." Dread curdled in Anna Kate's stomach at the thought that her aunt might have some ties, after all, to the salty sailors she'd run into at Port Gibson. "I, ah..."

Her aunt arched her brows impatiently. "Well, speak up, child! I don't have all day."

Anna Kate opened her reticule and withdrew the letter she'd retrieved at gunpoint. "I encountered a pair of sailors at Port Gibson. They asked me to give this message to you."

Her aunt swiftly rolled her wheelchair across the room to snatch up the letter. "Did you open it? Did you read it?"

Anna Kate frowned. "Of course not! It was addressed to you."

"Did the men say anything to you about the contents of the letter?" the woman pressed feverishly as she ripped open the envelope with a surprising show of vengeance.

"Not a word." Anna Kate shivered at the memory of their leering smiles and the way they seemed to be purpose-fully leading her away from the more populated area of town. "Then again, I didn't give them much of an opportunity. I was too suspicious of their intentions." She lifted her pistol from her reticule to emphasize her point.

Her aunt's agitation fled. She threw back her head and cackled loudly. "I can see that you and I are going to get along famously."

Anna Kate smiled back. It was a relief to discover that her aunt didn't mind it one bit that her niece was toting a pistol around her beautiful home. "Does that mean you're going to share what's in the letter I risked life and limb to deliver to you?"

Her aunt sobered. "In good time, my dear. In good time." Folding the piece of paper back in its envelope, she tucked it inside her pocket.

ANNA KATE FOUND HERSELF IMMERSED IN INVENTORY ledgers and vendor correspondence the very next morning. Her aunt had not been jesting about the number of letters she was required to write in the course of running her rail business. There were suppliers with which to negotiate the prices of goods. There were stagecoach and wagon drivers to handle deliveries. There were investments in various property holdings to manage. There were even written complaints to resolve — passengers who experienced delays in their travels, vendors who didn't care for the rise in commodities prices since the start of the war, an occasional injury that was occurred in the line of duty, and the list went exhaustively on and on.

"Do you honestly write back every person who contacts you?" On the third morning, Anna Kate slumped against her chair, massaging her tired writing fingers. A dark spot on one of them gave her pause. *Oh, dear!* She peered closer at her forefinger. It was an ink stain, one that wasn't in a hurry to come off no matter how much she rubbed it. She would have to speak to Nell about mixing a concoction to help get rid of it.

In three days, she'd spent more hours than she cared to count at the lovely roll-top desk in the corner of her aunt's office. The room was nearly as big as their library back home in Atlanta. The walls were lined with shelves bearing whimsical odds and ends that her aunt had collected from her many travels, stacks of papers, and books — not books to be read for pleasure like poetry or mythology, but many years worth of ledgers and records documenting her railroad and shipping transactions.

Aunt Win did most of her work at a throne of a desk in the center of the room. It was a wide, L-shaped workstation full of drawers and flat wooden pullouts to extend her work-space as needed. A writing area with an ink well and pen held down one end of the desk, while two sets of shelves with endless cubbyholes was perched on the other end. It was there that Aunt Win pored over maps of rail lines, routes, shipping schedules, and more. She was forever updating the documents and sending the changes to her key business associates.

Additionally, Aunt Win stayed in contact with a steady stream of couriers. They rode on horseback to and from her home nearly all hours of the day, not even ceasing at nightfall.

Or until Aunt Win hosted a party, apparently. Like magic, the courier visits halted at noon on Friday.

"Well, dear?" She looked up from her desk in the center of the room and finally pushed back her wheelchair. "I say we should call it a successful first week of work together."

Anna Kate, who'd been looking forward to the end of the work week all week, was almost too tired to answer.

"It's time to start preparing for our dinner party, my dear," her aunt continued cheerfully.

Anna Kate stifled a yawn as she laid down her pen. Now that the time of the party was nearly upon them, she wasn't certain she felt up to spending the rest of her day entertaining guests — not after a grueling week of work like the one she'd just experienced.

Her aunt chuckled. "Nell is busy drawing you a bath, and there's time for a nap if you'd like to indulge in one."

A nap sounded heavenly. "If you're certain there is time." She muffled a second yawn behind her hand.

"Of course there is," the woman declared with asperity. "I always take a short nap before these kinds of events. How else is a woman supposed to regale her guests with razor-sharp wit and musical wizardry after a long week of work?"

Anna Kate giggled at the mental picture her aunt's words created. "Very well. I'm off to freshen up and rest." She traipsed across the room to deliver a kiss to her aunt's cheek.

Aunt Win's expression softened. "Go along with you now, love."

ANNA KATE WAS AMAZED AT HOW WELL RESTED SHE felt after her bath and nap. She wasn't normally one to sleep mid day, but maybe her crotchety aunt was on to something. She put on a new party dress she hadn't yet had the opportunity to wear. It was a pale blue silk gown edged in delicate white lace at the neckline and wrists.

By the time she glided into the great room, a dozen or more guests were already milling and chatting.

"My darling niece!" her aunt crowed from her wheel-chair, where she was holding court in the center of the room. "Come! I am anxious to introduce you to my friends."

A glance around the room proved Will and Grady slinking out a side exit. Anna Kate caught Will's eye and gave him a warning look. He returned it with a lopsided grin and an unconcerned shrug, not at all bothered about leaving the socializing up to her. Grady didn't bother looking up as he kept moving. Though Anna Kate was well aware of their abhorrence for parties, she wished they might have seen fit to stick around a little longer for the first one. She wondered what they had going on this evening that was so much more important than supporting their sister's debut into San Antonio society.

"This is Zach Peterson, love." Interrupting Anna Kate's inward fuming, Aunt Win affectionately tugged her hand to bring her closer to her side. "And this lovely belle from Georgia is my dear niece and newest business partner, Anna Kate Monroe." The smile she beamed up at her niece was infused with pride and adoration.

Anna Kate flushed with pleasure as she faced her aunt's friend. "What my aunt is trying to say is that she's worked my fingers to the very bone in less than a week." She fluttered her fingers in the air for emphasis. Thankfully, Nell had succeeded in helping her remove all trace of the ink stain.

Those standing nearest them burst into companionable guffaws.

Zach Peterson caught Anna Kate's fluttering fingers and brought them to his lips. He was a broad-shouldered rancher, as brawny as a bear, with wavy auburn hair and an easy smile. "Anyone who can keep pace with the General for an entire week is made of stern stuff, indeed."

"The General, eh?" It was a fitting title for her demanding boss. Anna Kate nodded ruefully at her aunt, who gave one of her delighted cackles in response. "Someone might have warned me before I accepted the position."

Within another ten minutes or so, the room became crammed with people, and the party escalated to full swing. Apparently, her aunt's idea of a dinner party did not involve a sit-down meal in a formal dining room, but rather a lengthy buffet table weighed down with light finger foods, delicacies, and too many desserts to count. It was presided over by no less than four uniformed servants, who were constantly refilling the entrees and bringing out new ones.

Anna Kate peeked around the room every few minutes but failed to catch a glimpse of Gregory Armstrong. As the evening wore on, her disappointment about his absence grew. She'd been so looking forward to seeing him again.

"Looking for someone, my dear Miss Monroe?" Zack reappeared, bearing two glasses of golden cider. He held one out to her with a smile of satisfaction, as if certain that he was the one she'd been seeking out.

"In truth? I am," she confessed.

"Oh?" He cocked an eyebrow playfully.

"Yes. He's an investor my brothers and I met on our journey to Texas." She took one last sip of her cider, frowning thoughtfully as she set her half-empty glass on the tray of a passing servant. "My aunt invited him tonight for the express purpose of discussing the Santa Fe line."

"I see." Zack swirled his beverage before taking another drink. "In my experience, those stodgy tycoons in their middling years are an unpredictable breed."

He was staring into his glass, so he didn't see her eyes widen in surprise and mirth.

She couldn't pinpoint the exact moment Gregory Armstrong had entered the premises, but he'd somehow made it across the great room and was now standing directly behind Zack Peterson. From his smirk, she deduced he'd overhead the cowboy's colorful description of him.

She drank in his dark good looks, thrilled that he'd arrived at long last. Before she could greet him or make introductions, however, her aunt's hired pianist duo played their opening notes and launched into a cheerful dance tune.

With his cider glass still in one hand, Zack looped an arm Anna Kate's waist and twirled her towards the center of the room. Servants were busy pushing back chairs to clear it for dancing.

Gregory followed them with an amused curl to his upper lip. He watched for several minutes from the side-lines, even breaking into a few solo dance steps at one juncture.

Anna Kate watched him, laughing so hard she missed a step and nearly upturning Zack's glass of cider.

Gregory, who was in the process of sashaying his way to her side, neatly swiped the glass from her partner to save her dress from ruin. Then he cut in on their dance by returning the glass with a flourish to the startled Zack.

"I don't know who you think you are, mister," the cowboy sputtered, waving his glass of cider so furiously that he nearly tipped it over again.

"The stodgy tycoon," Gregory supplied, dancing Anna Kate a few steps away. While the man's jaw was busy dropping, he finished whisking her to the opposite side of the dance floor.

"That was wicked of you," she reprimanded when she was able to stop laughing long enough to speak again.

"It was," he agreed with a shameless smile. "Though I do recall warning you I would cut in if you failed to save me a dance."

"It was the first dance," she protested, still chuckling. "You really didn't give the fellow a chance."

He shrugged, not looking overly repentant. "Something tells me a proper southern belle like yourself will come up with a suitable punishment for my lapse in manners."

"In due time," she assured, allowing her eyes to twinkle up at him. It was so good to see him again, better than she imagined. She wasn't certain how such a thing was even possible on such short acquaintance, but she'd actually missed him the past few days.

He was taller than she remembered, more tanned, more handsome, more everything. And the way his dark eyes were caressing her back made her think there was a chance he'd missed her a little bit, too.

"How was your first few days on the new job, Miss Monroe?" he inquired after a short pause.

"I survived." She shook her head. "But don't let my Aunt Win's wheelchair fool you. Apparently, she's known as the general around this town. I have the tired fingers and shoulder blades to prove it."

"Did you deliver the letter from Port Gibson?" The fierce concern mirrored in Gregory's gaze made her catch her breath.

"I did."

"And?" he prodded gently.

"And nothing. She refused to share its contents, saying she would do so when the time was right."

His arms tightened around her. "Perhaps it's early in

our acquaintance to bare my soul in such a manner to you..."

When he paused, she hardly dared to draw another breath. Was the dashing Gregory Armstrong about to declare his feelings for her? The lights in the room danced dizzily overhead as lightheadedness swept through her.

"Yes, Gregory?"

His mouth twisted in a grimace while he gazed deeply into her eyes. "I reckon I'd like to think you'd feel safe coming to me if you ever needed to — for any reason. A shoulder to lean on. A confidante. A help in time of need."

That certainly wasn't what she'd been expecting him to say, but his words thrilled her all the same. "I would feel safe. I *do* feel safe when I am with you."

"Good. I am glad." The smile he bestowed on her did not entirely erase the wrinkle of worry from his brow.

The music to the first dance drew to its jaunty conclusion, as the last resounding notes were played.

A ringing of a fork against a glass created a lull in the many conversations taking place across the room.

"Your attention, please! Your attention, please!" It was Zack Peterson ringing his glass. His eyes glittered with banked fury as they came to rest on Gregory. "A courier just arrived with an update from the battlefront."

As if being doused with a bucket of ice cold water, the chattering around the room ground to a shocked halt. Everyone strained to listen, several crowding closer.

"The Confederacy has passed the Conscription Bill. Any man between the ages of twenty and forty-five may be called to arms." Zack's gaze passed bleakly over the room. "We all knew this day was coming. It is time to get our houses in order. Time to prepare ourselves for what's next."

Chapter 5: Gathering Evidence

May, 1862

Over the next month, Gregory called on the Monroes often enough to become a regular fixture at their dinner table. At times, he was consumed with guilt over the knowledge that the kind-hearted family presumed his reasons for ingratiating himself into their lives was because he was courting Anna Kate, which he supposed he was.

He'd not kissed her yet nor declared his feelings for her outright, but he could no longer deny how drawn he was to her, nor how enamored. The attraction was there, and it was mutual. She teased and sassed him to no end, but he could read what was really happening in her sea-blue eyes. He could see the joy that sparked in her features each time he appeared at her aunt's front door, and he shared the happiness she exuded each moment they were able to seize alone.

They took long walks across her aunt's ranch property and spent many enjoyable hours in the gazebo overlooking the rear courtyard. He could also tell that she approved of the number of times he rode horses with her brothers and took them on short hunting expeditions.

"How long?" she inquired softly one afternoon.

He dropped his gaze, knowing what she was asking. How long was he going to stay in Texas? How long did they have left together? It was a topic his higher ups hadn't given him permission to discuss with her and probably never would. Since they hadn't yet named a precise deadline, he gave her the most honest answer he could. "I do not know."

They were sitting together on a bench in the gazebo, half facing each other. It was quiet enough outside that he could hear the distant roar of the falls — water gushing from a tall crevice between the mountains and plunging into the spring below it. He wanted to ride with her there someday, to take in the beauty of the waterfall together.

Her hand crept across the small space between them, making him drag in a breath of wonder when her warm fingers curled inside his. "You are a man of many secrets," she observed quietly.

"Much to my regret." He didn't enjoy the necessity of keeping secrets from her. There was an unspoken understanding between them, a well of heartfelt regard that made him wonder if there was a chance she might actually forgive the truth about his true vocation if she ever discovered it. Though he knew it was strictly forbidden to confide such things in her, he longed to share his true mission in the Union Army, his real identity as a northern spy, and his genuine feelings for her. He was falling in love. There was no more point in denying it or fighting it.

But despite his occasional bouts of wallowing in hopeless longing, he was forced to admit the likelier truth — that Anna Kate would never agree to court a man in his line of work. Until the war was over, he could see no hope for their relationship.

"I understand more than you think I do." She squeezed his hand. "I'm the daughter of a railroad executive. There were more things Papa couldn't confide in me about his business dealings than what he could confide in me. Mostly because of the war, I presume."

Yes? His ears perked up, straining to hear more, but she did not elaborate. Disappointed, he announced vaguely, "The war changed a lot of things for a lot of people."

"But especially for our family." There was no mistaking the sadness in her voice. It tugged at his heart.

"Oh?" he prodded.

She reached up to tuck a strand of hair behind her ear. "It's the whole reason Papa sent me and my younger brothers west. He lives in the hope that the fighting will never reach this far. That we'll be safe here until the war is over."

He could only hope and pray that was the case. "You must miss them terribly." Though he was trained to make leading statements, which would hopefully elicit useful information from his targets, Gregory found himself doing what he always did with Anna Kate — asking her questions out of genuine concern for her wellbeing.

"I do. I cannot wait until the day our family is reunited." Tears prickled at the edges of her eyes, wrenching his heart-strings. Though he'd endured the hardships of war, he found his heart unable to resist the tears of the woman he loved.

"Perhaps they can visit here for the holidays?" It was a foolish proposition, considering his inside knowledge about the Union Army's forthcoming raids on every railroad spur leading south. If the war lasted long enough, all trade and shipping between the Union and Confederate states would cease, along with most personal travel back and forth via the railways.

She shook her head, blinking to keep her tears at bay. "It isn't likely. Although Papa has never owned a slave and abhors the practice, he's a southern man through and through. Georgia is our home. Keeping the railways up and running through Atlanta is his way of protecting what's ours. He'll not be taking a vacation until the fighting is over."

Gregory nodded in quiet understanding. For weeks now, he'd suspected this was her family's stance on the war, but it was good to finally hear the admission from her own lips. Perhaps there was yet hope that he could help her family dodge the treasonous allegations being made against them. Just because they owned and operated a rail line did not mean they had any direct involvement in the shipping of weapons and other war supplies. He was torn between relief at the notion of clearing their name and distress at the knowledge that doing so would end his current assignment in San Antonio.

"Oh, fiddle!" Anna Kate exclaimed suddenly, wrenching her hand from his.

He stared in surprise, missing the warmth of her fingers.

"I almost forgot. One of our couriers was ill this morning, so I agreed to carry my aunt's latest batch of letters to the post office." She jumped to her feet. "I've chattered nearly my entire lunch hour away. Pray forgive my abrupt departure, but I must be on my way."

He stood and crooked his arm at her. "May I drive you into town? I was heading that way myself."

"You are too kind," she waved his hand away, "but I'd

best summon Rupert. Otherwise, you'd have to bring me back afterward."

"Do you really think I'd mind that, Anna Kate?" His voice dropped to a tender note.

She caught her breath and seemed to be having trouble meeting his gaze. "I, er..."

"Then it's settled. We'll continue our conversation on our way into town." He reached for her hand and tucked it around his forearm, liking how good her hand felt there. How right.

Minutes later, she was perched next to him in his buggy. It was a two-seater with the top down, hitched to a brown gelding and a golden mare. The gelding had a white starburst on his forehead, while the other horse had a white stripe running from the top of her head to the tip of her nose.

Anna Kate's gaze sparkled as she leaned closer to the glossy horses. "What are their names?"

He chuckled. "The one on the right is Star, of course."

"Of course," she murmured.

"The one on the left is Merriment."

"What a charming name for a horse!" She wrinkled her nose. "Is there a story behind it? She appears rather docile in nature for such a colorful name."

"I reckon there is, but I didn't have time to ask when I rented her from the livery this morning."

She lifted her blonde brows suggestively. "We could spin our own story."

His gaze dropped momentarily to the pack of letters resting in her lap. "Our story would probably be more thrilling than the truth."

"Of course it would be. I'll start us off." She shot him a mischievous look. "There once was a lonely debutante from the deep south. The reason she was lonely was because she loved to dance and sing, play the pianoforte, and attend parties with her friends. But a group of dragons flew in from the north, threatening her entire town and everyone in it. It forced the debutante to stay indoors so much that her beautiful home began to feel more like a prison."

Gregory's shoulders tensed as he realized Anna Kate was telling her own story.

"Her name was Merriment, because of how much she liked to party. However, the siege of the dragons forced her to spend endless hours at her easel, painting watercolors of the countryside she was no longer free to roam."

As they rolled past miles of cacti and Joshua trees against a backdrop of craggy canyons, Gregory wished more than anything that he'd met his lovely companion under different circumstances — in a place where there was no north or south, nor any dragons or wars.

Her nudge against his ribs jolted him from his melancholy. "It's your turn. We're supposed to be spinning our tale of Merriment *together*, remember?"

"I haven't forgotten." He grinned down at her, longing to swoop his head a little lower to sample her rosy lips. "So Merriment sat beside her second-story window, gazing at all the birds and beasts on the other side of the wall, wishing she was as free as they were. Though the dragons had ravaged their way through the chickens and goats, there were certain creatures they dared not touch for fear of being cursed."

"I'm intrigued." Anna Kate clasped her hands over the letters in her lap. "Which beasts inspired such fear and respect in the dreadful dragons?"

"The wild horses, of course." He reached over to flick a finger against her nose. "It was because the leader of their herd wasn't just any regular ol' horse. He was a unicorn with special powers that the dragons were very much afraid of."

"Like what? Could he fly?" Anna Kate gave an impatient bounce in her seat.

"That's a good question. I believe it's your turn to take over the story, Miss Monroe." Gregory settled back in his seat to continue driving while her musical voice washed over him. He allowed himself the luxury of pretending, just for a few minutes, they were man and wife on their way to go shopping. He would take her out to lunch afterwards at one of the local cafes and order her the nicest meal on the menu. Afterward, he would—

"Ow!" A pinch on his arm made him straighten in his seat.

"Wake up!" Anna Kate commanded with a chuckle. "Else you'll miss the end of my masterful tale."

"I wasn't asleep," he grumbled, hating to let go of his pleasant daydreams.

"Your eyes were drifting closed. We could have run into a prickly cactus or worse," she chided severely.

He laughed. "I think the only prickly cactus in sight is the one sitting next to me."

She tossed her head, pretending she hadn't heard him. "As it turned out, the unicorn's special power was that of a shapeshifter. Once every seven years, he could change places with any living creature of his choice. It was usually a difficult decision, but not this time. The moment the unicorn spotted Merriment weeping beside her bedroom window, he trotted closer. A twitch of his nose made the moon shift across the sky and eclipse the sun. Shocked by the sudden burst of darkness, Merriment shot to her feet and threw open her window sash. Within the shadows of the eclipse, the dragons failed to see how ripe she was for the plucking." She paused and glanced over at Gregory for his reaction.

"That's a cruel place to end a story." He shook his head at her. "Pray assure me that the sad young woman didn't get eaten."

"Of course not, because the unicorn chose that moment to change places with her. There." She dusted her hands. "I got us to the rousing climax. You are the one who must finish it to the sweet or bitter end."

A fresh wave of melancholy rolled through him at the thought that there would be no sweet ending for him and the real Merriment, only a bitter one. It was such a depressing thought that he ended their story with haste. "Alas, the eclipse ended so quickly that the unicorn girl didn't have time to close her bedroom window before the dragons noticed it was open. Quick as a flash, one of them swooped from the sky and plucked the body of the sad young debutante from her home — never realizing it held the spirit of a unicorn — and carried her far away, never to be seen again."

"Good heavens!" Anna Kate gasped. "Please assure me they did not dine on her. I said you could finish our story with a sweet or bitter end, but I did not agree to outright carnage."

Outright carnage. Gregory's upper lip curled at the irony of her words. Such were the fruits of war. There were no real winners in the end — nothing but carnage to clean up when the last cannon finished smoking. In the case of the current war, he was fairly certain that most of the carnage would be wrought in the south, since that was where most of the battles were being fought.

"Well, don't stop now!" Anna Kate protested. "You

must finish the story, Gregory Armstrong, lord of the sordid tale of Merriment."

Lord Gregory Armstrong. His face whipped to hers, trying to gauge if she was teasing or if she'd somehow learned one of his deepest secrets. An ancestor of his had been a duke from London. Thus, the title had been passed down for six generations, and now it belonged to him. He most often claimed his military title of captain. Nevertheless, he still legally held the claim to his English title. The beachside estate he'd inherited lay in near ruins on the Massachusetts coastline, overgrown and vacant. Someday, after he'd served his last assignment in the Union Army, he intended to go claim and restore what was rightfully his.

He stonily met her gaze, longing to find the unthinkable there — her love and acceptance in spite of her discovery of who he really was.

Her lovely eyes sparkled back at him with mischievous intent. "I'm waiting," she reminded, crossing her arms and drumming her fingers impatiently. "For the ending of our story, sir."

His hope vanished, as it dawned on him that she'd merely called him "lord" in a playful sense. "Well," he drawled, swallowing his sadness and forcing his thoughts back to the plight of their fictitious heroine. "Merriment loved her freedom as a unicorn so much that she never wanted to shift back into the lonely young debutante she'd been before. Fearful that her old body might survive the dragon abduction and return to switch places with her again, Merriment hid in the woods until a wizard came along and helped her change her appearance to that of a regular horse. Her horn become a long white stripe running down the center of her head all the way to her muzzle."

"Just like the horse you rented, eh?" Anna Kate chuckled.

"Oh, my story is better than that. She's one and the same horse," he declared cheerfully. "You see, even though Merriment assumed the appearance of a horse, she was actually still a unicorn. And as everyone knows, unicorns are magical creatures who can never die, so she lives happily on."

Anna Kate clapped her hands in delight. "You, my dear Gregory, are a truly marvelous storyteller!"

My dear Gregory. Blast it all, but he wanted to be exactly that! Her dearest friend and more!

"Alas, the post office is in sight, so we shall have to spin our next tale together another time."

He drew abreast of the weathered storefront building and leaped down to tether his horses. What he planned to do next was the antithesis of courting the woman he loved. Though subterfuge was his job, it felt dishonest and blackhearted to employ it with Anna Kate. Nevertheless, duty called. If he didn't gather some evidence soon to prove or disprove that the Monroe family was in direct communication with the Confederate Army, his superiors would pull him from the assignment and send him elsewhere. That he could not allow. Unable to bear the thought of being permanently separated from the woman who held his heart in her hands, he did the unthinkable.

He reached for her and lifted her down from his buggy.

Her cheeks turned the most delectable shade of pink, and her lips parted on a silent gasp as her gaze met and clashed with his.

Feeling like the lowliest cad for taking advantage of such a sacred moment, he flicked the edge of her packet of letters and sent them tumbling to the ground.

The thin string they were tied with came loose, and they scattered like leaves. A light breeze caught the edges of the envelopes and made them dance and skip along the ground.

"Oh, no!" Anna Kate dove after them, her skirts flapping around her ankles as she collected them as fast as she could before they blew away.

"Pray forgive me!" Gregory cried, hating the lie he was living. "I must have bumped them. I should have been more careful."

"It's not your fault, silly man." She squealed and made a flying leap to catch one errant envelope with the toe of her boot before it whirled away. "Good gracious! That was a live one!"

While stooping to assist her, he managed to slide one of envelopes into the pocket of his trousers without her noticing.

She was laughing and out of breath by the time they retrieved the final envelope, none the wiser about the one he'd secreted in his pocket. To his relief, she made no attempt to count them to determine if any were missing.

Two hours later, he had his elbows propped on the trestle table in his boarding house room, poring over the letter by the sunlight pouring through the window. What he read made his blood run cold, especially since it was recorded in the handwriting of his beloved.

No! This can't be right! An hour earlier, he'd been so sure Anna Kate was innocent that he would've bet his life on it. However, evidence to the contrary stared back at him, as clear as the three o'clock hour that was gonging from a church tower in the distance.

He'd been skillfully trained in the art of encryption, and whoever had composed the note had employed one of the oldest and simplest ones of all time, the Caesar Cipher. It was a simple shift, though the user had attempted to make it more difficult by shifting the key by one additional letter with each consecutive word. In the end, their cleverness was no match for his own. He swiftly decoded the garbled words: NPSF became the word MORE after a single shift. UQNFKGTU became the word SOLDIERS after a double shift. DPPXQLWLRQ became the word AMMU-NITION after a triple shift. LWPG became the word JUNE after a shift of four letters. TSJ became the word ONE after a shift of five letters. The completed message was clearly a military directive: *More soldiers, ammunition June 1st.*

It was with a heavy heart that Gregory dragged his boots to the telegraph office to report his first significant finding since his arrival in San Antonio. Guilt flooded his chest at the knowledge that telling the truth meant betraying the Monroe family. It was a bitter pill to swallow, considering how dear they'd become to him.

The message Gregory sent to his superiors resulted in his immediate recall to Boston, as he knew it would. He didn't have the heart to concoct a dishonest farewell to Anna Kate and her family, knowing their fate hinged directly on his honor as a man and a soldier — neither of which he had much confidence in these days.

He truly had no idea if he would ever see her again. Knowing a clean break would be best for them all, he hardened his heart and boarded a train without looking back.

Chapter 6: A Weary Traveler

February, 1863

O ver the next several months, Anna Kate struggled to accept the fact that Gregory had left town without saying goodbye. Deep in her heart, she'd always known he would leave. He'd stayed long past the number of weeks he'd originally allotted for his trip. Still, leaving her without a word of warning made no sense.

Her heart wept a thousand tears in her bed at night as she considered every possibility — each one more horrific than the last. What if he'd been attacked by outlaws? What if he'd been taken prisoner by the dreaded Yankees? What if he was lying sick or injured in some lonely stretch of desert between San Antonio and wherever he'd headed next? She visited the post office several times per week, craving news of his whereabouts, but none came. All she had to cling to were the terrors of the unknown.

Her brothers stomped around their aunt's vast ranch home in a righteous fury on her behalf. "If I ever catch sight of that cad again, I'll flatten his face," Grady snarled for the hundredth time.

Anna Kate flinched with each well-meaning threat her brothers issued. She didn't want Gregory's face flattened. She wanted the brush of his fingers against hers. She wanted his delicious dark eyes drinking her in. She wanted, more than anything, to hear his husky baritone surrounding her, assuring her, and making her feel safe again.

Aunt Win watched Anna Kate in tight-lipped worry as she worked in silence, without complaint, painstakingly writing out each letter that was dictated to her. She watched in growing alarm as her niece began to skip meals, claiming she was resting and eating in her room; but the wait staff reported the truth back to her — that her niece simply had no appetite and returned most of her trays to the kitchen untouched. She lost weight and her gowns grew loose.

"You have to eat something," Aunt Win finally exploded. "It's been months, child. He's not coming back."

Anna Kate felt the color leave her face, knowing they were speaking of Gregory. "He will, Aunt Win. I know he will." *He cares for me, and I care for him. He will not stay gone forever. He simply can't!*

"Oh, my darling," her aunt sighed. "We all adored him. We truly did. But for reasons we do not understand, he chose to leave."

"But what if he didn't choose?" Anna Kate's voice quavered. "What if he was made to go against his will?" *Like I was in Port Gibson?* "Perhaps we should have filed a missing persons report with the sheriff. Do you think it's too late to do so?"

Aunt Win muttered something unintelligible and continued to write. She finally paused, lifted her paper into the air, and waved it to dry the ink. "I am throwing a dinner party on Friday in honor of William's twentieth birthday. It will be just like the old days. That means you *will* put on one of your lovely dresses, and you *will* attend it."

Her demeanor reminded Anna Kate so much of the dueling banty roosters in their pen out back that she chuckled.

Aunt Win's head whirled in her direction. "Did I hear what I think I heard?"

Anna Kate only laughed harder. Her aunt's cautious smile faded, as Anna Kate's mirth soon dissolved into hysteria. With it came the tears she'd been fighting for so long to hold back.

"Oh, my dear, sweet niece!" her aunt groaned. She wheeled her chair from around her desk and rolled across the room toward Anna Kate. "Come now." She patted her shoulder. "I cannot make the hurt go away, but I'm sturdy enough to cry on."

Anna Kate wilted wordlessly against her shoulder, weeping uncontrollably. She drenched the fabric of her aunt's upper sleeve, unable to stop until there wasn't an ounce of energy left to heave out another sob.

"I love him so much," she rasped, way too distressed to keep the truth to herself any longer.

"I know you do, precious." Her aunt's voice was so choked with emotion that Anna Kate realized she was weeping, as well.

"You love him, too." The last word ended in a hiccup.

"Yes, child."

Her aunt's admission was far more soothing than her brothers' endless string of rants and threats. "Thank you for saying that, Aunt Win." Anna Kate let out a rueful chuckle. "It helps somehow. I don't know why. It just does."

Her aunt nodded and unearthed a handkerchief to dab

at her eyes. "I'm still hosting that dinner party for your brother, mind you, and you are still required to attend it."

"If you insist." Anna Kate smiled through her tears. "I have just the dress in mind for it."

I T   W A S   D I F F I C U L T   T O   D O N   A   P A R T Y   G O W N   W H I L E   H E R heart was so heavy. After her crying bout on her aunt's shoulder, however, Anna Kate felt obligated to try harder for her family's sake. Her aunt still needed an assistant, and her brothers still needed a sister. Will was serving as an apprentice down at the shipping yard, learning all there was to learn about the day-to-day operations of keeping a railroad line running. He often discussed and debated his newly acquired knowledge with her in the evenings. She looked forward to their chats, since she was still learning the administrative side of the business.

Grady was attending school and occasionally required her assistance with his homework. He was a whiz at computations, but not so much with correspondence. It simply wasn't possible her to quit being a sister to either of her brothers, no matter how much her heart was breaking.

A half hour before the dance, she stood in front of her dressing mirror and eyed her eggplant hued gown. Her skin was so pale these days, the color of the fabric made her look like a ghost. "This will never do," she muttered. Though it was February, it was southern Texas, which meant the temperatures would be in the upper sixties or thereabouts by the time the party began in the afternoon. Not to mention, her aunt was notorious for overheating her home with a fire in every hearth.

Throwing caution to the wind, Anna Kate pushed

deeper into her wardrobe and selected a pale pink silk. Anyone who wished to criticize her gown for being out of season was free to do so. She required a cheerful color if she was going to make it through the party, and that was that!

Using a tray of cosmetics, she dabbed and powdered her features into some semblance of good health. Then she applied the lightest sheen of red to her lips and cheeks. The result was a young woman in the mirror who looked a bit more like her old self, albeit she wasn't able to completely erase the shadows from beneath her eyes.

Will gave a long, low whistle as she glided up the hallway toward the great room. "If I'd have known my birthday would unearth such a fetching creature, I would have started celebrating a month ago." He held out his hand. "I believe I'll claim your first dance for myself. You might be my sister, but you'll still be the prettiest girl in the room."

She chuckled and placed her hand in his.

When they entered the great room together, their aunt glanced up from her circle of friends. Her well-practiced social smile widened to one of immense pride. "Here's the birthday boy!" she cried, clapping her hands.

A flick of their aunt's wrist made the stringed quartet in the corner of the room strike the opening notes of their first number. Without missing a beat, Will led Anna Kate onto the dance floor. They performed a lively waltz that inspired several other couples to join in. At the end of the dance, Zack appeared to claim her hand.

Will yielded his sister with a gallant bow.

The rancher looked less rugged this evening. For one thing, his auburn hair was clipped shorter. His face was leaner, too. Anna Kate tried not to stare, but it was difficult. The changes in him were so remarkable that he almost looked like a different man.

"I dropped some weight," he finally muttered.

"Why? Are you well?" she asked anxiously.

His eyebrows rose. "Would you care if I wasn't?"

"Of course I would! What sort of question is that?" She gaped at him, wondering what she'd said to put him out of sorts. "Aren't you in a surly mood this evening, my friend?"

"I don't want to be your friend," he growled. "I thought I made that clear on a number of occasions."

"Zach," she sighed.

"Just hear me out." His lips twisted bitterly. "I stepped aside to make room for that blasted tycoon a few months ago, thinking that was what you wanted. I never imagined he'd be fool enough to leave you behind like this. Please know I would never abandon you in such a callous manner if you belonged to me."

"He'll come back." Anna Kate had no idea where the words came from, only that they were true. Her biggest regret at saying them aloud was the disappointment they were sure to bring to Zach. However, it couldn't be helped. Her heart belonged to another.

"And if he doesn't?" Zach ducked his head to bring the two of them to eye level. "I am still here. That is all I want you to know."

"You are very kind to say that, Zach." The music transitioned to a slower dance that made her heart constrict with sadness. Anna Kate didn't mind sharing the faster jigs with her brother and Zack, but the slow dances she'd always reserved for Gregory in the past.

She disengaged herself from Zach's embrace with a lowered gaze, fully intending to slip from the room before attracting any more dance partners.

"May I have this dance?"

Her heart stuttered a beat at the familiar voice. It was

one she'd longed to hear again, but didn't quite believe she ever would. Then a set of warm, very familiar hands closed possessively around her waist.

"Gregory?" she breathed, feeling faint as she slowly raised her gaze to his. "Is it really you?"

His tanned features were more sharply chiseled than she remembered, his eyes an agonized shade of ember. "I couldn't stay away. I had to see you again."

"Oh, for crying out loud!" Zack groaned. "You're back?" His auburn head swiveled between the two of them. When neither looked his way, he threw his arms up with a huff of defeat and backed away.

For several moments, Gregory's handsome features danced dizzily in front of her.

"Anna Kate." He shook her lightly. "Are you well? May I fetch you a drink?"

"Don't you dare walk away from me!" she hissed between clenched teeth. "You have a powerful lot of explaining to do!" Her eyes grew damp.

"And I will, darling. I promise." He glanced anxiously around them and steered her to a curtained alcove.

Darling. The tenor of his voice and the way his eyes burned into hers made her heart unravel further.

The moment they were safely ensconced behind the velvet curtain, his arms came around her, cuddling her close.

"I feared the worst," she choked against the lapel of his dark suit. "I couldn't eat. I couldn't sleep."

"It is entirely my fault, and I beg your forgiveness," he muttered against her temple. "I'll never forgive myself for the agony I must have put you through. It was wrong. *I* was wrong."

"Just tell me what's going on," she begged, leaning back

in his arms to look up at his face. "What made you leave me, and what kept you away?"

"I cannot." His voice broke. "I know that is the worst possible answer to your questions, but it is the truth, my precious girl. I have sworn my allegiance to powers greater than myself, and my secrets are not my own to give away. Not even to the woman I love."

His words made her shudder and burrow closer. "Is it true, Gregory? Do you love me?"

"More than my own life." He tipped his forehead against hers. "And that, quite possibly, is what my return trip to you will cost me."

What? It was impossible to read his expression with their noses pressed together and his mouth hovering over hers. "Other than your confession of love, you speak in riddles."

When he raised his head from hers, what she saw in his eyes shook her beyond words. It was a love so desperate that it spilled over her, surrounding her and holding her captive beneath its spell.

She slowly raised herself on her tiptoes, until her mouth was a breath away from his.

"We cannot, Anna Kate," he whispered hoarsely. "That is, I am not at liberty to—"

She silenced him by pressing her trembling lips to his.

With a groan of surrender, he crushed his mouth to hers. "I do not deserve this or you," he muttered against her lips. "I will never deserve you."

GREGORY KNEW HE HAD NO RIGHT TO DISOBEY ORDERS like this — no right whatsoever to detour southwest on the trip he was supposed to be making to Utah. However, he'd been unable to help himself. If he'd been unable to lay eyes on Anna Kate again soon, he would surely have expired.

Seeing the sadness in her eyes and how much weight she'd lost was almost enough to rip his heart in two, especially knowing he was the cause of her distress.

By the time he raised his head, both their faces were drenched in tears. "I disobeyed orders by coming here," he confessed. "My superiors will send someone to fetch me, and I will have to face the consequences."

His words made her heart race painfully. "Who exactly are your superiors, Gregory Armstrong?"

"I am not at liberty to say, but this I can tell you." He grimaced. "No matter what punishment they decide to mete out, seeing you again was worth it."

Her heart melted at his words. "Anyone who would punish you for paying me a visit isn't worth serving," she declared fervently. "There is no need for you to await punishment. We will leave town together." She gripped his shoulders. "My family's wealth will take us anywhere in the world. We can catch a ship overseas if we want."

He cupped her face in his hands. "If only I could, my precious girl. Believe me when I say there is nothing I want more than to remain at your side, but it's not safe. My presence will bring you nothing but trouble."

She flung her arms around his neck and tugged him down for another kiss. "I am not afraid of trouble, Gregory. If there are dragons to face, we will face them together."

He kissed her slowly and tenderly, basking in a brand of love he didn't deserve from a woman whose smiles would surely turn to glares if only she knew the truth about him.

"Come with me." She reached for the glass paneled door behind them, turned the handle, and pushed it open.

He was amazed to see they'd been standing by a door all this time. He'd mistakenly presumed it was a window.

She led him outside to the gazebo where they'd spent so many happy hours in months gone by. By the time they ascended the stairs, she was shivering with cold.

"You'll catch your death out here." He unbuttoned his jacket and tossed it around her shoulders.

"Then we'll find a different place to talk. Let's keep moving." She tugged him across the gazebo and down the opposite set of stairs. A minute later, she flung open the carriage house doors. "Here. This is better, so long as you don't mind the dark." She led him to her aunt's carriage. "We can sit here for a spell."

He assisted her into the cushioned seat and joined her, leaving the door ajar. She snuggled against his side. "Someday you're going to tell me everything, Gregory Armstrong."

"I want to." He spoke against her temple. "I never wanted to keep secrets from you. Please believe me when I say it eats away at me, day and night."

"Then I will share my secrets with you, instead." She reached up to palm his cheek.

No, please. An agonizing crack formed in the center of his heart and started to splinter downward. Anything incriminating she confessed to him about her crimes or the crimes of her family, he would be oath bound to report to the Union Army. "You don't need to tell me anything," he choked.

"I know, but I wish to. Something tells me that it is the right time."

Horror gripped his chest.

"I once told you that my father never owned a slave, did I not?"

"Yes," he grated out, scrambling for an excuse to halt her confession.

"Well, my oldest brother, Jackson, is an outright Union sympathizer. I reckon our whole family is when it comes to the bigger issues at stake in our country. For this reason, Jackson wanted us to flee to the Blue Ridge Mountains to wait out the war in seclusion. There are pockets of men and women living up there who hate the fact that our state seceded from the Union."

"Unbelievable." The tightness in Gregory's chest eased. "Tell me more, darling." Exhilaration swept him at the realization that the love of his life was not only handing him back his own life, she was also handing him back hers. Her heart was good. He should have trusted his instincts from the beginning.

With the solid intelligence she proceeded to spill into his ears, he might very well be able to barter his way back into the good graces of his superiors. With any luck, they'd assume he'd followed a last-minute lead to Texas instead of deserting his post like the love-sick suitor that he was.

Anna Kate was able to reveal no less than three settlements populated with Union sympathizers. He'd send word about them to his superiors at first light. If their investigation proved fruitful, there was no telling how many more recruits they'd have — inside enemy lines, no less — to join the cause of liberty and justice for all.

He hugged her closer, rejoicing in the fact that God was still on His throne and there was mercy still to be had this side of glory, after all.

"When the war is over, darling, will you marry me?"

She gasped and tipped her face up to his. "Yes, my precious Gregory, I will."

"Thank you." He kissed her tenderly. "May the end of our nation's struggles come quickly."

A breathy chuckle escaped her. "There is one more struggle you must face tonight, I'm afraid. Two, actually."

He touched her cheek, knowing she was speaking of her brothers. "I'll have a word with Will and Grady before I go."

IN THE END, IT DIDN'T TAKE NEAR AS MUCH convincing as Anna Kate imagined it would to get her aunt and brothers to forgive Gregory for his lengthy absence.

"I am deeply sorry." He faced them with his head bowed and his hat in his hands.

"Sorry doesn't begin to cover it, mister," Will exploded. "If you expect to prance back into our lives, we need answers. Why did you leave? Where have you been? And why did you come back?"

"I cannot discuss those things," he returned quietly. "I truly wish I could, but I cannot."

"He's a federal marshal," Anna Kate blurted.

"Anna Kate!" Gregory protested, looking aghast.

"One who's working undercover," she lied, "and he is not allowed to breathe a word about it. I guessed it on my own."

"Oh, Anna Kate!" he groaned. "What are you doing, sweetheart?" He looked so stricken that she had to wonder how close her fabrication was to the truth.

She held his gaze, daring him to contradict her. "Either that, or he's been lying to me all along and he's actually an outlaw. Or a pirate," she teased.

He shook his head, his gaze taking on a wicked glint as

she continued to bait him. To her disappointment, however, he made no effort to correct even her wildest claims.

Something about his faint northern accent and his inability to speak a word about his true identity still didn't add up, but she loved him enough to keep her word and marry him when the war was over — so long as they were both still standing.

Chapter 7: Conscripted

June, 1863

Anna Kate and her brothers settled back into some semblance of normalcy. This time, however, she was boasting an engagement ring on her finger. It was downright distracting trying to write her aunt's correspondence all day with the lovely square diamond winking up at her. Whatever Gregory did for a living must be lucrative, because the ring on her hand must have cost a fortune.

Her evenings were filled with visits from Gregory, dinner parties, musicales, games of cards, and starlight trysts with him in the gazebo. Her aunt allowed it so long as one of her maids remained within sight at all times. Anna Kate could not remember a time in her life when she'd ever been happier.

Until the dreadful letter from home arrived.

Will was at his apprentice job, and Grady was at school. If it weren't for the war, Anna Kate would've waited until they were home to read it. However, the news from home might be of an urgent nature, so she couldn't afford to wait.

"Is everything well with my brother and Jackson?" Aunt Win inquired curiously from behind her desk in the office.

"Indeed, I hope so." Anna Kate anxiously scanned the lines of her father's letter.

My dearest Anna Kate, Will, and Grady:

I trust this letter finds you and your aunt well. By now, you've surely heard about the Conscription Bill that was passed by the Confederacy a year ago. Well, the day we've long feared has arrived. Jackson, Will, and I have been drafted into service. We have thirty days to report to duty, so it is best that Will begins his journey back to Georgia as soon as you receive this letter. I do not wish for him to be charged with dereliction of...

"No!" Anna Kate gasped, tossing the letter on her desk. "We will not send Will to join a war our family does not fully believe in."

"Why, Anna Kate!" her aunt protested. "I understand your sentiments about the Conscription Bill. What I do not understand is your outburst against your own government."

"Pshaw!" She rolled her eyes. "You do realize that the Union doesn't even recognize our secession, do you not? If the north wins the war, and it is beginning to look as if they will, the Confederacy will cease to exist." She was no longer an empty-headed debutante. During her aunt's parties, she'd been keeping her ears tuned in to every piece of news she could gather about what was happening on the front lines.

"This is our land. Our home, love. Why would you not want to defend what is ours? What will be yours someday?"

Anna Kate smiled. "You sound a lot like Papa."

"And what is wrong with that?" her aunt returned with alacrity.

"Nothing at all, my dear aunt," Anna Kate assured. "Now if you will excuse me, I must speak with Gregory about Will's situation."

"Your father wants him on the next train back to Georgia, love. I am not sure what there is to discuss."

"Even so, ma'am, I'd like to inform Gregory what is going on." She didn't bother telling her aunt that she had no intention of following her father's orders in this matter. He and Jackson were hundreds of miles away. Even if they came to fetch Will themselves, she would have a week or longer to come up with a way to protect him from the Conscription Bill — for good.

With that in mind, she borrowed her aunt's driver and carriage and flew across town to the boarding house where Gregory was staying.

The front desk clerk hurried to fetch him, and he materialized on the stairs, hurrying down them to greet her. "What is wrong, Anna Kate?"

She whipped out the horrid letter and shoved it in his hands. "Read this, and tell me what I should do."

GREGORY SCANNED THE CONTENTS AND IMMEDIATELY understood the cause of her agitation. It moved him greatly to know she'd come to him with her troubles. He already knew she loved him, but this proved she trusted him, as well.

"I will not send him, Gregory! He is too young," she snapped.

He arched a brow at her. "Will is twenty, darling." He'd

been younger than that when he first joined the Union Army.

"Fine!" Her lips tightened. "Perhaps he is old enough. I still do not wish to send him."

He shared her sentiment, having no interest in supplying yet another soldier to the southern cause. "I have an idea."

"Good." She clasped her hands expectantly beneath her chin. "I can't wait to hear it."

"It's going to cost you, sweetheart." He steered her towards the dining room on the main level.

"How much?" she asked suspiciously.

"My price is the time it takes to share a lunch with me."

Her lips twisted ruefully. "Now that you mention it, I haven't eaten all day."

"Then we will order soup, while I share my plan to save Will."

The dining room was fairly crowded, but they managed to secure a table for two on the far side of the room.

"Perfect," Gregory noted in satisfaction.

A waitress sailed in their direction with a pitcher of lemonade. Instead of soup, she coaxed them into ordering pot roast and steamed vegetables. By the time she moved away to fill their order, Anna Kate's mouth was watering at the thought of the feast that was on its way.

She and Gregory sipped on their lemonade for a minute. Then he set down his glass. "Will is going to have a horrible disfiguring accident on his job," he announced in a flat tone.

"He is?" Her eyes widened. "I beg your pardon, but did I miss your opening lines?" she mocked. "Is this another story like the one about the unicorn named Merriment?"

"A bit like that, except this one has a much happier

ending." He reached across the table to rest his hand atop hers. "Do you trust me, Anna Kate?"

"With all my heart." She blew him a kiss.

It was all he could do not to lean across the table and claim her lips right then and there. He wanted to, though — badly.

"Quit looking at me like that," she hissed, blushing. "One look at you, and anyone will guess what you're thinking."

He didn't share her embarrassment. Far from it. On the contrary, he hoped every man and woman in the room could take one look at his beloved and know that she belonged to him, forever and ever.

"I know someone who can forge medical papers for your brother and send a report back to the Confederate Army about this horrible, crippling accident I previously mentioned. I assure you, darling, the southern army will not want his services after they read the report."

Anna Kate nodded in approval. "A year ago, I would have told you I hated lying as much as the good Lord does, but I am willing to do whatever it takes to keep Will safe." She lowered her voice. "It would be different if they were asking him to fight for a cause we believe in, but..." She shook her head. "Everyone I know finds the practice of slavery utterly repugnant. I cannot support a cause that would keep such an immoral and unconscionable practice in place."

AUNT WIN, AS IT TURNED OUT, WAS NOT ONLY delighted to hear of Gregory's plan, she was a willing accomplice in mailing the forged papers. In the end, they did not so much as notify Will of his conscription. If he was ever interrogated, he could sincerely deny knowing a thing about it.

Alas, a second letter arrived from Jack Monroe a few days later, notifying them that Jackson had been forcibly conscripted in the middle of the night. The hooded, masked representatives from the Confederacy had additionally informed Jack that his own conscription orders had been cancelled, most likely because they needed him to keep the railroad running.

"They are monsters, every last one of them," Anna Kate snarled through gritted teeth. Tears streaked her face at the thought of the many dangers Jackson would be facing in the coming days — poor, honorable Jackson, who'd never supported the war in the first place.

The men who'd snatched Jackson hadn't bothered telling Papa where Jackson was being sent, either. It could be Virginia, South Carolina, or any number of other places — meaning it could be a very long time before they found out if Jackson was dead or alive.

April, 1864

By some miracle, Gregory's superiors saw fit to leave him in San Antonio as the war dragged on. They were amazed at the intelligence he continued to dig up from a post so far west of the fighting. Meanwhile, he continued intercepting letters dictated by Anna Kate's aunt and selectively feeding information to the Union Army that did not directly point back to the crotchety old lady.

The hardest part of his days, however, was supporting

Anna Kate each time she received a letter from home describing how desperate things were becoming there.

"So far, Papa has received only one letter from Jackson," she lamented to him one evening over dinner.

"I am sorry to hear it." They were sitting beside each other in her aunt's dining room, so he reached under the table for her hand. He inwardly vowed to go search for her brother at the next available opportunity. In the meantime, he could telegraph a few discreet inquiries to a few contacts who might be able to locate a missing soldier.

"Papa says things are getting worse each day in Atlanta," she sighed. "I wish he and Jackson had come west with the rest of us."

Gregory squeezed her hand in sympathy. Now that the north was blocking nearly all trade in the southerly direction, the availability of food and supplies was growing tighter and tighter in the southern states. This had led to the Confederate forces instigating yet another emergency bill, one was even more unpopular than the practice of conscription — impressment. This allowed their troops free license to take whatever they wanted from whoever they wanted, which included crops, fuel, and a slew of other commodities. For the first time in the history of Monroe Industries, Jack reported he was barely breaking even. He was at great risk of losing money in the upcoming weeks and months.

"'I'll increase my shipments to Jack." Aunt Win laced her gnarled fingers together as she leaned heavily on the dinner table. "We Monroes have seen hard times before. We'll get through it like we always do, with hard work and perseverance."

Gregory nodded, unable to meet her shrewd gaze directly. Alas, due to the intelligence he continued to pour to his superiors, her shipping routes would not be in operation much longer. By now, he'd determined exactly which routes coming out of Texas were being used to ship fighting men, ammunition, and other supplies to the Confederate front lines. It was only a matter of time before the Union shut them down, once and for all.

He'd finally proven that Jack Monroe and his four children were in no way responsible for the alleged crimes against their nation. Aunt Win, on the other hand, was not so innocent. Not only was she in direct communication with a few high-ranking southern officials, she was issuing steep discounts on their orders for supplies at the cost of barely breaking even herself.

But that was far from the biggest problem facing the Monroes right now. Thanks, in part, to Gregory's own efforts, Atlanta was now a high priority target of the Union Army. The city was a major rail and supply center for the Confederate troops, which meant it had been marked for destruction. He needed to figure out a way to get Jack Monroe out of town before the Union troops struck.

Chapter 8: Traitor Among Us

July, 1864

"I must have a traitor in my company," Aunt Win announced crisply one afternoon. "I've known it for some time. I just didn't want to believe it, though the truth has been staring me in the face."

"Why, Aunt Win! Whatever do you mean?" Anna Kate paused her writing and laid down her pen.

"It started off with little things, love. Letters that I know I dictated to you and I know you recorded for me, but they never arrived to their intended destinations."

"What?" Anna Kate gasped. "Surely you do not believe I was negligent in my duties!"

"You? No." Her aunt gave a bark of dry laughter. "I wish I could say the same for that handsome beau of yours."

"You think Gregory is at fault? How?" A lump of sickness formed in the pit of Anna Kate's stomach. They were suspicions she'd shared for quite some time now. Ever since he'd helped Will avoid the Conscription Bill, she'd known he wasn't an outlaw or a pirate. A man who wielded that kind of power had friends in high places. Or, as was more likely in his case, reported to officials in high places.

"Why would you say that, dear?" Her aunt peered over her spectacles with an expression that gave no indication about her thoughts on the matter. She was wearing one of her workaday brown dresses and looked very much the part of a spinster. "I seem to recall you saying he's a federal marshal."

"I know what I said," Anna Kate said quietly.

"To protect him?" her aunt prodded. "Or because you truly believed it to be the truth at the time?"

"You don't?" Anna Kate tried to sound nonchalant, but wasn't sure if she'd succeeded.

"No, I do not." Aunt Win removed her spectacles and laid them carefully on her desk. "Something tells me you don't believe it, either."

"I love him, Aunt Win." That was the one thing she was sure about.

"I know, dear."

"And he loves me, too."

"Yes."

"He loves our whole family. He would never do anything to harm us," Anna Kate said desperately.

"You want to believe it, and I want to believe it; yet there's the matter of all my missing letters to consider." She spread her hands. "Along with all of my seized shipments. And what about that blasted northern accent of his?" Aunt Win folded her too-thin arms over her gaunt chest, pursing her lips in consideration.

"What exactly are you trying to say, Aunt Win?" Anna Kate's voice shook. She didn't want to hear it, but she couldn't bring herself to stand up and leave the room.

"Trust me, child, I did plenty of digging before coming

to the conclusion that Gregory might not be everything he seems." Her aunt looked suddenly exhausted. "I telegraphed a half dozen or more inquiries to contacts I have in the north."

"In the north!" Anna Kate frowned in concern. "Why?"

"To ask about a certain Gregory Armstrong. Funny how no one seemed to know a blessed thing about Gregory Armstrong, the railway investor, but they knew quite a lot about Captain Gregory Armstrong. He is a well respected man, as it turns out, in the *Union* forces."

"A captain, you say?" Anna Kate felt faint. It made a dreadful sort of sense, now that her suspicions were confirmed. It would explain so many things — from his secrecy to the inner battle he always seemed to be fighting with himself.

"He's also a duke. A somewhat impoverished one, mind you." Her aunt sniffed. "Apparently, he inherited some dilapidated homestead along the coastline of Massachusetts from that part of his family tree."

"Are you certain of this?"

"My sources are deadly accurate, niece."

"But that would make the man I love a—"

"A northern spy," a familiar male voice intoned from the doorway.

"Gregory!" Anna Kate jolted in shock, half-rising from her seat. "Say it isn't true. Please say it isn't true."

"I cannot, my dearest Anna Kate." Though he sounded heartbroken, his grim expression held a note of relief, as well.

"Don't call me your dearest!" she cried, wondering what part of him could possibly be relieved about her discovery of such a dastardly secret about him. So much for the blind trust she'd placed in him again and again! In return, he'd betrayed her and her family in nearly every way possible. What in the world was he planning, and why had he kept it a secret for so long? Her blood chilled at the possibilities.

"Do you hate me now that you know?" His face paled as his eyes burned into hers.

"I should," she quavered. "Just tell me one thing. Are you the person who intercepted my aunt's letters?"

"I am."

"And delivered them to the Union Army?"

"I did."

"Then, yes. I completely and utterly despise you." It wasn't true, of course. She hated what he did for a living, but she wasn't sure that she was capable of ever hating him. She couldn't say the same for him, however.

She sank weakly back into her chair as everything that he'd left unsaid washed over her. He'd used her in the worst way possible, pretending to love her just so he could get closer to her aunt's business. Had any of what had transpired between them been real?

"Anna Kate!" her aunt said sharply. "He is also the man who saved Will and who is working very hard, as we speak, to get your father out of Atlanta before it's too late."

"Too late for what?" Anna Kate's head swiveled between the two of them. Then the truth sank in. Because of her unwitting assistance in helping the man she loved gather intelligence against the south, the Union forces were going to attack Atlanta. She sagged forward in her chair. *I will not swoon! I will not swoon!* Too much was at stake, not the least of which was her father's safety.

Gregory shouted something and lunged in her direction, but she was quicker. She reached for her reticule beneath her desk and yanked out her pistol. "Not another step!" she cried in a shaky voice.

95

"Don't shoot, Anna Kate!" her aunt sounded horrified. "Please don't do it. You'll regret it for the rest of your days."

"He betrayed us, Aunt Win, in every way. Atlanta will fall because of him. Papa is going to die..." She paused, hardly able to finish the sentence. She swallowed hard, forcing the words past numb lips. "Papa is going to die because of him." She cocked her pistol and aimed.

"No, my dear. Gregory did not betray us entirely. It is my firm belief that your papa is going to live because of him," her aunt assured in quiet, clipped tones.

Anna Kate's gaze flicked back to her. More than anything, she wanted to believe what she was hearing, but her heart was too shattered to summon that kind of hope. It was over for the Monroes. Why couldn't Aunt Win see that?

Her aunt held her gaze without wavering. "I'll admit that the man you love has followed his conscience and fulfilled his duty as a northern soldier. However, he only did so after first seeing fit to extract your father. If my sources are correct, dearest, Jack Monroe boarded a train for San Antonio two days ago."

Anna Kate's vision blurred. The pistol slid from her nerveless fingers and fell with a thud to a stack of papers on her desk. The room felt like it was spinning.

"So I fell in love with a northern spy?" she asked faintly. It was so much worse than her many theories about marshals, outlaws, and pirates. All northern sympathies aside, it meant his comrades were right this second shooting at people she cared for — her friends, the boys she'd grown up with, people like Jackson!

As she turned her angry gaze in Gregory's direction again, tears scalded her cheeks and dripped down her chin, dampening the high neckline of her dress.

"I fell in love with you in return." If Gregory's eyes burned any brighter, they would burst into flames. "With every ounce of my heart, strength, and intellect. It has consumed me from the inside out most days, making me question my loyalties and my very honor."

She stared at him, lips parted. The fact that he seemed to think a few flowery words could make things go back to normal between them was downright ludicrous. "I used to think love was enough," she choked, "but I was wrong." It felt like eons ago that she'd embraced such innocence. Such utter nonsense.

"Anna Kate! You don't mean that!" He took a step toward her.

"In light of everything that has happened, I think you should leave," she informed him coldly. Yes, she still loved him, but that would be her cross to bear in the coming days. No matter how badly they might wish it wasn't so, the two of them were on opposite sides of the war. They always had been. They'd been working at cross purposes the entire time they'd known each other.

"I am more sorry that words can articulate." His eyes were dark with torment. "I never meant to hurt you like this."

"But you did." She tried to lift her chin to exhibit a brave front, but the room started swirling again. This time, everything went black.

Chapter 9: What Her Heart Wants

Anna Kate's heart ached when she awoke. She knew without asking that Gregory was gone. It chilled her to the bone to know that he wasn't coming back this time. She'd seen to that. Her angry accusations at him were still ringing in her ears. *Mercy!* She'd gone as far as to tell him that she despised him.

The look he'd given her afterward was seared into her heart forever. It would torture her to the end of her days.

Aunt Win rolled into the room with a cup of hot tea. "You're awake at last." There was a sigh in her voice that tugged at Anna Kate's heartstrings. Clearly, her aunt had not been unaffected by Gregory's duplicity.

"I, er…" She sat up in bed, hugging the quilt to her chest with one hand as she accepted the cup of tea.

"You don't have to say anything." Her aunt's voice was gentle. Her gnarled hands rested above the wheels of her chair, ready to spin around and depart.

"But I want to," Anna Kate blurted. She needed to get some things off her chest, and she knew her aunt would listen.

"Then we'll talk." Aunt Win reached out to run a hand over the wrinkled folds of the quilt, waiting.

Anna Kate blew on her tea to cool it. "How can you be so calm about everything?" All it would take was a few strokes of Gregory's pen to send her aunt to prison, or worse. Most likely worse.

Aunt Win pointed upward, making the bracelets on one hand jingle. "I have faith, my dear."

"But we're losing," Anna Kate quavered. Everyone with sense knew the southern states would soon be beaten, and then what?

Her aunt shrugged. "No one was ever going to win this awful war. Not really." Her voice was sad. "The Good Book says that a house divided against itself cannot stand. The same is true of a country. The cost to both sides of the fighting is steep. Too steep." Her voice broke. As the first tear trickled down her wrinkled cheek, Anna Kate knew her show of emotion was for all the lost lives and limbs. It was for all the men — young and old, northerners and southerners — who would never return home to their families again.

"Is even a small part of you afraid?" Despite her aunt's tears, Anna Kate still couldn't detect any fear. Only dull acceptance of what was coming.

"Not unless Gregory has figured out the whole truth about me, which I suspect he has, and blows my cover, which I suspect he will not." Her voice was matter-of-fact.

Anna Kate abruptly transferred her cup of tea to the nightstand. "Why are you speaking in riddles all of a sudden?" Her throat tightened painfully as one reason sprang to her mind.

Her aunt drew a deep breath and let it out slowly. Her gaze dropped to a loose thread on the quilt that she was twirling around and around. "Has it yet occurred to you that Gregory might not be the only person in your inner circle who's been at war with himself?"

Anna Kate studied her aunt for a shocked moment. "I can only presume you're referring to...you?" Her voice rose to an incredulous squeak.

"I am, dearest." Aunt Win drew a shuddery breath. "I hardly know where to begin, so I'll simply dive into the heart of my story. Even Gregory doesn't know what I'm about to tell you. I'm sure of it."

"Know what?" Anna Kate whispered.

"I got caught. That's what." Her aunt raised her gaze once again, revealing eyes that had taken on a bruised and weary cast. "I won't say how or when, since I've been sworn to secrecy on those details. I've already said more than I was supposed to. But, everything considered, you deserve to know the truth, and here it is. Like Gregory, I'm not one hundred percent the woman you think I am," she concluded with a sigh of regret.

"Of course you are!" Anna Kate fisted her hands in the quilt. She couldn't believe what she was hearing. "You're a good person and an honest one. An America patriot through and through, and I love you for it." Not to mention she was her beloved aunt, confidante, and friend. She was also the closest thing to a mother she'd had in a very long time.

"Yes. I am an American." Her aunt latched onto that word like it was a lifeline. "The man who caught me in the act of smuggling supplies to the southern troops was quick to remind me of it, too. Ever since then..." She paused to clear her throat. "Ever since then," she continued, "I have been shipping supplies, while knowing a good amount of them were being intercepted and redirected, er... elsewhere."

"North?" Anna Kate gasped out the word.

"I cannot say." More tears trickled down her aunt's cheeks.

"Can't or won't?" Anna Kate bit out the words. Her mind swirled with confusion. If her aunt was saying that she'd been serving both sides of the war, then she'd been arming the very troops that were firing at her own brother and nephew. It was truly mindboggling.

"Both." Aunt Win reached up to wipe the tears from her face. "I cannot say, since I do not know for sure, nor would I be at liberty to tell you if I did know."

Anna Kate nodded, hardly knowing what to say. After a long pause, she rasped. "I think I'd like to be alone for a bit." What she'd learned was a lot to absorb. It was almost too much to absorb. She no longer knew what to think or even feel. Her insides had grown numb.

"I understand, dearest." Without any further ado, Aunt Win wheeled her chair around and left the room.

Anna Kate spent the next couple of hours weeping, praying, and weeping some more. After the numbness in her heart finally wore off, she was forced to accept the fact that she still loved her aunt and Gregory deeply. Yes, she was furious with both of them. She was hurt, too, but she still loved them. She would always love them.

Telling Gregory that she despised him couldn't have been further from the truth. She loved him so much and so hard that the pain radiated straight through her body and soul.

Which did nothing to save her hometown.

Thanks to her aunt's impeccable sources, they were notified only a handful of days later that Atlanta had fallen.

And just like Captain Gregory Armstrong had promised, Jack Monroe showed up on Aunt Win's doorstep a mere few hours after news of the fateful event reached them.

Anna Kate made it to the door first. She took one look at her father's ravaged features and held out her arms to him. "You're home."

No other words were necessary between them as he took her in his arms and held her like he was never going to let her go again.

Christmas

ANNA KATE'S TWENTY-THIRD BIRTHDAY CAME AND went, and the Great War finally ended. The Monroes immediately fell into a frenzy of plans to go hunt for Jackson, whom they'd not heard from for too many months to count.

They sent dozens of telegrams, called in every favor from every contact between Texas and Georgia, pored over maps, and plotted out the places they would travel to search for him. Their intended destinations included hospitals, boarding houses, and another venue that none of them could bring themselves to say aloud — cemeteries.

The Monroes withdrew scads of money from the bank, purchased enough medical supplies to tend to an entire unit of soldiers, and packed their travel bags and trunks.

Since they were scheduled to depart Christmas morning, they gathered on the front lawn to load Aunt Win's carriage. Before they could take off, however, a lone buggy appeared on the horizon. It was drawn by a pair of dark horses. As it drew closer, Anna Kate could make out the silhouettes of two figures. Men, from the looks of their top hats.

"Get behind me, Anna Kate." Papa waved her back and stepped forward to stand shoulder-to-shoulder with her brothers, weapons drawn and pointed at the approaching buggy.

"Jackson?" Grady blurted in an astounded voice. He shaded his eyes for a closer like. "It's Jackson, Papa." He lowered his weapon and started jumping up and down, waving wildly and hollering, "Jackson!"

One of the men in the buggy lifted a hand and waved back.

"Who's that driving him?" Will asked curiously. "It's hard to tell with how far the brim of his hat is pulled over his eyes."

It's him!

Anna Kate's heart thudded with a mixture of wonder and dread. She didn't have a clear view of the buggy because of her position behind her father, but she knew without looking who it was — who it *had* to be.

"It's Gregory," she intoned softly. "I'd bet my life on it." Their long overdue confrontation was the only explanation that could unravel the mess she called her heart these days. It was the only thing that could turn everything in the world that was wrong back to right.

Stepping around her father, she faced the approaching buggy, knowing Gregory must be bringing her the one peace offering he knew she would accept — her oldest brother. She didn't know how he'd done it and could only imagine the lengths he'd gone to make it happen, but he'd persevered.

For me.

Her family grew still as the two men pulled in front of

Aunt Win's home. It was like watching a miracle unfold in front of them.

The front door of the ranch house flew open. "What in tarnation?" Aunt Win abruptly stopped talking, struck to silence by what she saw.

Jackson emerged from the buggy unassisted. Well, unassisted by human hands, that is. Once he was on the ground, he pulled a set of crutches from the buggy and leaned heavily on them as he swung himself in their direction. When he was a few strides away, they could see his leg wasn't merely broken. The left one was missing altogether below the knee. He was pale but jubilant as he lifted a crutch and waved it at them.

"Welcome home, soldier." Papa's voice cracked as he stretched his arms wide.

Jackson hobbled straight into them. Will and Grady crowded closer, wiping their eyes and mumbling words of love. Anna Kate threw her arms around them all, overwhelmed with the joy of knowing her oldest brother was alive. The Monroes were back together again.

After a while, Jackson reached for her to pull her deeper into the family huddle, pressing her cheek against his shoulder. "Still as pretty as a peach, I see."

And he was as rakishly handsome as ever, despite the missing part of his leg. Mercy, but the ladies were going to sigh and swoon over him, just as soon as they realized there was a war hero in their midst. Anna Kate was certain of it.

While Papa and her younger brothers plied him with endless questions about his military exploits, she slipped away from them to face the man who'd made their family reunion possible.

He was waiting for her beside the buggy. Her eyes

clashed with his dark searching ones as she glided slowly in his direction. Her heart pounded with every step.

"You came back," she said shakily.

"Nothing could have kept me away." He pushed his hat farther back to get a better look at her. "I had to see you one more time, but I'll leave if you want me to."

"I don't want that." A tear streaked down her cheek at the realization that the Lord had seen fit to give them another chance. This time, she wasn't going to foolishly throw it away. "I don't want you to leave again," she choked. "Ever!" She was done being prideful and angry. She was more than ready to make things right.

"Are you sure of that, Anna Kate?" He handed the reins of his horses to Rupert, who materialized out of nowhere. "Because if you take me back, sweetheart, there will be no getting rid of me this time." He swiveled determinedly in her direction. "I have no plans to ever again leave Cedar Falls. Or you."

He held out his arms to her.

Laughing and crying at the same time, she launched herself at him, knocking off his hat as he lifted her from the ground to swing her around and around. She rained happy kisses all over his face — his forehead, his nose, his cheeks, and, at last, his mouth.

His lips were tender and cherishing. "I love you," he whispered huskily. "I never stopped, even when there was no reason to keep hoping."

"I never stopped loving you, either." She anxiously searched the harsh angles of his face. "You know that, don't you? Though I said some truly awful things the last time we —mmm," she sighed against his mouth as he claimed her lips once more.

"Prove it," he taunted, tightening his arms around her, "by marrying me."

"Are you asking me to, er...?" She was unable to finish the question.

For an answer, he let her go and took a knee in front of her. "I am. There's nothing that would make me happier than if you'd agree to be my wife, Anna Kate. I want to spend this Christmas with you and every Christmas afterward."

"I want that, too, Gregory. So very much," she answered shakily.

He stood and took her in his arms again. "Merry Christmas, sweetheart. I love you."

"Merry Christmas, Gregory. I love you, too." She tipped her face up to his to seal their newest promise to each other with another kiss.

Way down deep, it felt like the start of something beautiful and precious — a merging of the old and the new, the east and the west, and — in time, Lord willing — the north and the south.

Cedar Falls was certainly a wonderful place in the country to start fresh, away from the carnage of war. Anna Kate's mind was already spinning with dreams of putting down roots and staying right where they were. It was a topic she planned to bring up with Gregory soon. Very soon. She hoped he would consider it.

But for today, she was going to enjoy just being together. Never before had Christmas felt more like Christmas, because she finally understood why love is called the greatest gift of all.

Lawfully Witnessed

Thank you for reading
Lawfully Witnessed.

Are you ready to dive into the adventures of our next bride in trouble? As first, it's flattering to have a man delivering gifts to her doorstep every morning. But when he starts pressuring her to marry him, she worries he might be more interested in her recent inheritance than her.

Start reading book #2 in the
Brides of Cedar Falls Series.
It's called
Wanted Bounty Hunter
A sweet historical holiday romance with a light twist of suspense!

Sneak Preview: Wanted Bounty Hunter

A *wealthy heiress hires a rugged bounty hunter to pose as her fiancé in this sweet and swoony opposites-attract historical romance!*

Thanks to a lavish inheritance, Rachel West can finally afford to follow her dreams and open the Cedar Falls Finishing School for Young Ladies. Unfortunately, a former co-instructor from Boston follows her to her hometown, claiming a deathbed promise to look after her. All too soon, he's pressuring her to marry him, making her fear he's only interested in getting his hands on her money.

Bounty hunter Boone Cassidy is accustomed to far more dangerous assignments than helping a spoiled rich girl discourage an unwanted suitor — even one with a string of bad debts and a bounty on his head. He fully expects the snobby headmistress to send him packing the moment she catches sight of his dark skin and rough and tough exterior. Instead, an unexpected attraction ignites, making him dream about impossible things like happily-ever-after with the woman who writes his paycheck.

Grab your copy of
Wanted Bounty Hunter
Available in eBook and paperback on Amazon + FREE in Kindle Unlimited.

Note From Jovie

Guess what? I have some Bonus Content for you. Read a little more about the swoony cowboy heroes in my books by signing up for my mailing list.
There will be a special Bonus Content chapter for each

new book I write, just for my subscribers. Plus, you get a FREE book just for signing up!

Thank you for reading and loving my books.

Jovie

Sneak Preview: Cowboy for Annabelle

To protect her from a ruthless set of debt collectors, an impoverished southern belle agrees to become the mail-order bride of a rugged cowboy.

After refusing to marry the cruel new owner of her childhood home, Annabelle Lane finds herself on the run from the scoundrels he hires to change her mind. In desperation, she signs a mail-order bride contract and hops on the next train, praying the groom she is matched with is a man worth running toward.

The most sought-after range rider in the west, Ethan Vasquez is highly skilled at protecting livestock from bears, wolves, and rustlers. But it's a job that leaves no time for courting, no matter how determined he is to have a family of his own someday. When a dare from friends has him scrambling to send off for a mail-order bride, he never imagines how quickly she will arrive or how much trouble will follow. It's a good thing he knows a thing or two about handling predators. He can only hope she finds his heavily scarred hands worth joining with hers in holy matrimony after the first wave of danger is past.

Grab your copy of
MAIL-ORDER BRIDES ON THE RUN #1:
Cowboy for Annabelle
Available in eBook and paperback on Amazon + FREE in Kindle Unlimited.

Complete trilogy — read them all!
Cowboy for Annabelle
Cowboy for Penelope
Cowboy for Eliza Jane

Join Cuppa Jo Readers!

If you're on Facebook, you're invited to join my group,
Cuppa Jo Readers. Saddle up for some fun reader games
and giveaways + book chats about my sweet and swoony
cowboy book heroes!

https://www.facebook.com/groups/CuppaJoReaders

Sneak Preview: Elizabeth

Early November, 1866

E lizabeth Byrd rubbed icy hands up and down her arms beneath her threadbare navy wool cloak as she gingerly hopped down from the stagecoach. It was so much colder in northern Texas than it had been in Georgia. She gazed around her at the hard-packed earthen streets, scored by the ruts of many wagon wheels. They probably would have been soft and muddy if it weren't for the brisk winds swirling above them. Instead, they were stiff with cold and covered in a layer of frost that glinted like rosy crystals beneath the setting sun.

Plain, saltbox buildings of weathered gray planks hovered over the streets like watchful sentinels, as faded and tattered as the handful of citizens scurrying past — women in faded gingham dresses and bonnets along with a half-dozen or so men in work clothes and dusty top hats. More than likely, they were in a hurry to get home, since it was fast approaching the dinner hour. Her stomach rumbled out a contentious reminder at how long it had been since her own last meal.

So this was Cowboy Creek.

At least I'll fit in. She glanced ruefully down at her workaday brown dress and the scuffed toes of her boots. Perhaps, wearing the castoffs of her former maid, Lucy, wasn't the most brilliant idea she'd ever come up with. However, it was the only plan she'd been able to conjure up on such short notice. A young woman traveling alone couldn't be too careful these days. For her own safety, she'd wanted to attract as little attention as possible during her long journey west. It had worked. Few folks had given her more than a cursory glance the entire trip, leaving her plenty of time to silently berate herself for accepting the challenge of her dear friend, Caroline, to change her stars by becoming a mail-order bride like she and a few other friends had done the previous Christmas.

"Thanks to the war, there's nothing left for us here in Atlanta, love. You know it, and I know it," Caroline had chided gently. Then she'd leaned in to embrace her tenderly. "I know you miss him. We all do." She was referring to Elizabeth's fiancé who'd perished in battle. "But he would want you to go on and keep living. That means dusting off your broken heart and finding a man to marry while you're still young enough to have a family of your own."

She and her friends were in their early twenties, practically rusticating on the shelf in the eyes of those who'd once comprised the social elite in Atlanta. They were confirmed spinsters, yesterday's news, has-beens...

Well, only Elizabeth was now. Her friends had proven to be more adventurous than she was. They'd responded to the advert a year earlier, journeyed nearly all the way across the continent, and were now happily married.

Or so they claimed. Elizabeth was still skeptical about the notion of agreeing to marry a man she'd never met. However, Caroline's latest letter had been full of nothing but praise about the successful matches she and their friends had made.

Be assured, dearest, that there are still scads of marriage-able men lined up and waiting for you in Cowboy Creek. All you have to do is pack your bags and hop on a train. We cannot wait to see you again!

Caroline had been the one to discover this startling opportunity by reading an advert in The Western Gentle-men's Gazette. It had been placed there by a businessman who claimed to be running the fastest growing mail-order bride company in the west.

All I had to do is pack my bags and leave behind everyone and everything I've ever known to take part in the same opportunity. Elizabeth shivered and pulled her cloak more tightly around her. Attempting to duck her chin farther down inside the collar, she wondered if she'd just made the biggest mistake of her life. She was in Cowboy Creek several days later than she'd originally agreed to arrive, having wrestled like the dickens with her better judgment to make up her mind to join her friends.

Oh, how she missed the three of them! Caroline, Daphne, and Violet were former debutantes from Atlanta, like herself. All were from impoverished families whose properties and bank accounts had been devastated by the war. It was the only reason Elizabeth had been willing to even consider the foolish idea of joining them. She was fast running out of options. Her widowed mother was barely keeping food on the table for her three younger sisters.

Even so, it had been a last-minute decision, one she'd made too late to begin any correspondence with her intended groom. She didn't even know the man's name, only that he would be waiting for her in Cowboy Creek when her stagecoach rolled into town. Or so Caroline had promised.

With a sigh of resignation, Elizabeth reached down to grasp the handles of her two travel bags that the stage driver had unloaded for her. The rest of her belongings would arrive in the coming days. There'd been too many trunks to bring along by stage. In the meantime, she hoped and prayed she was doing the right thing for her loved ones. At worst, her reluctant decision to leave home meant one less mouth for Mama to feed. At best, she might claw her way back to some modicum of social significance and be in the position to help her family in some way. Some day...

Her hopes in that regard plummeted the second she laid eyes on the two men in the wagon rumbling in her direction. It was a rickety vehicle with no overhead covering. It creaked and groaned with each turn of its wheels, a problem that might have easily been solved with a squirt of oil. Then again, the heavily patched trousers of both men indicated they were as poor as church mice. More than likely, they didn't possess any extra coin for oil.

Of all the rotten luck! She bit her lower lip. *I'm about to marry a man as poor as myself.* So much for her hopes of improving her lot in life enough to send money home to Mama and the girls!

The driver slowed his team, a pair of red-brown geldings. They were much lovelier than the rattle-trap they were pulling. "Elizabeth Byrd, I presume?" he inquired in a rich baritone that was neither unpleasant nor overly warm and welcoming.

Her insides froze to a block of ice. This time, it wasn't because of the frigid temperatures of northern Texas. She recognized that face, that voice; and with them, came a flood of heart wrenching emotions.

"You!" she exclaimed. Her travel bags slid from her nerveless fingers to the ground.

———

Hope you enjoyed the excerpt from the
Mail Order Brides of Cowboy Creek #1:
Elizabeth
Available in eBook, paperback, and Kindle Unlimited on Amazon.

Complete trilogy — read them all!
Elizabeth
Grace
Lilly

Much love,
Jovie

Sneak Preview: Hot-Tempered Hannah

U nlike his name suggested, there was nothing angelic about Gabriel Donovan. Quite the contrary. While most men were settled down with a wife and family by his ripe old age of twenty-six, he preferred the life of a bounty hunter, tracking and rounding up men who carried a price on their heads. He extracted money and information and taught an occasional lesson to particularly deserving scoundrels when circumstances warranted it.

Most people kept their distance from him, and he was okay with that. More than okay. Making friends wasn't part of the job, and he sincerely hoped he didn't run into anyone he knew at the Pink Swan tonight. Unlike the other patrons, he wasn't looking for entertainment to brighten the endless drag of mining activities in windy Headstone, Arizona. If any of the show girls from the makeshift stage at the front of the room bothered to approach him, they'd be wasting their time. He'd purposefully chosen the dim corner table for its solitude. All he wanted was a hot meal and his own thoughts for company.

"Why, if it isn't Gunslinger Gabe," a female voice cooed, sweet as honey and smoother than a calf's hide. She plopped a mug of watered down ale on the table, scrapping the metal cup in his direction. "I's beginning to worry you wasn't gonna show up for your Friday night supper."

"Evening, Layla." He hated her use of his nickname. Hated how the printed gazettes popping up across the West ensured he would never outride the cheeky title. It followed him from town to town like an infection. He hated it for one reason: None of his eight notorious years of quick draws and crack shots had been enough to save his partner during that fated summer night's raid.

It was a regret that weighed down his chest every second of every day like a ton of coal. It was a regret he would carry to his grave.

He nodded at the waitress who leaned one hand on the small round table with chipped black paint.

"Well, what's it going to be this time, cowboy?" Her dark eyes snapped with a mixture of interest and impatience. "Bean stew? Mutton pie? As purty as your eyes are, I got other tables to wait on, you know."

The compliment never failed to disgust him. Along with his angelic name, he'd been told more times than he cared to count that he'd been gifted with innocent features. If he heard another word about his clear, lake-blue eyes that inspired trust, he would surely vomit.

"Surprise me." He hoped to change the subject. Both entrees sounded equally good to him. He was hungry enough to eat the pewter serving ware, if she didn't hurry up with his order.

Layla's movements were slow as sap rolling down the bark of a maple tree. "If it's a surprise you're looking for...." She swayed a step closer.

"Bring me both," he said quickly. "The stew and the pie. I haven't eaten since this morning."

"Fine." The single word was infused with a world of derisive disappointment. A few steps into her stormy retreat, she spun around. Anger rippled in waves across her heart-shaped face. "I know what you really want."

"You do?" The question grated out past his lips before he could recall the words. Sarcastic and challenging. It had been a rough day. The last thing he needed was a saloon wench to whip out her crystal ball and presume to know anything about his life. Or his longings. No one this side of the grave could fill the void in his heart.

"I sure do, cowboy." She was back in front of him before he could blink, her scarlet dress shimmering with her movements. "An' I can show you a real special time. Something you ain't never gonna find on no supper menu."

He didn't figure any good would come of trying to explain that his heart belonged to a ghost. Wracking his brain for a sensible way to end their conversation without offending her further, he stared drearily at his mug. There was no quickening of his breathing around any women these days. No increased thump of his heartbeat. Not like there had been with Hannah. His dead partner. Or Hot-Tempered Hannah, as she'd been known throughout the West.

Then again, maybe he wasn't completely dead yet on the inside. He felt a stirring in the sooty, blackened, charred recesses of his brain as his memories of her sprang back to life. Memories that refused to die.

His mind swiftly conjured up all five feet three inches of her boyishly slender frame stuffed in men's breeches along with the tumultuous swing of red hair she'd refused to pin up like a proper lady. Nor could he forget the taunting tilt of her head and the voice that turned from sweet to sassy in a heartbeat, a voice that had been silenced forever due to his failure to reach their rendezvous in time.

Lord help him, but he was finally feeling something alright — a sharp gushing hole of pain straight through the chest. He mechanically reached for his glass and downed the rest of his ale in one harsh gulp.

"Well, I'll be!" The waitress peered closer at him, at first with amazement, then with growing irritation. "I've been around long enough to know when a body's pining for someone else."

What? Am I that transparent? His brows shot up and he stared back, thoroughly annoyed at her intrusive badgering.

Layla was the first to lower her eyes. "Guess I'll get back to work, since you're of no mind to chat." Her frustration raised her voice to a higher pitch. "I was jes' trying to be friendly, you unsociable cad. I'll try not to burn your pie or spill your soup, since that's all you be wanting." Her voice scorched his ears as she pivoted in a full circle and stormed in the direction of the kitchen.

He stared after her, wishing he could call her back but knowing his apology wouldn't make her feel any better. A woman scorned was a deadly thing indeed. He could only hope she didn't poison his supper.

He hunched his shoulders over his corner table and went back to reminiscing about his dead partner. Known as Hot-Tempered Hannah throughout Arizona, she'd stolen his heart with a single kiss then threatened to shoot him if he ever tried to steal another.

He had yet to get over her. Hadn't looked at another woman since.

Jo Grafford, writing as Jovie Grace

Hope you enjoyed the excerpt from
Mail Order Brides Rescue Series 1:
Hot-Tempered Hannah
Available in eBook, paperback, and Kindle Unlimited on
Amazon.

This is a complete 12-book series.
Read them all!
Hot-Tempered Hannah
Book 2: Cold-Feet Callie
Book 3: Fiery Felicity
Book 4: Misunderstood Meg
Book 5: Dare-Devil Daisy
Book 6: Outrageous Olivia
Book 7: Jinglebell Jane
Book 8: Absentminded Amelia
Book 9: Bookish Belinda
Book 10: Tenacious Trudy
Book 11: Meddlesome Madge
Book 12: Mismatched MaryAnne
Box Set #1: Books 1-4
Box Set #2: Books 5-8
Box Set #3: Books 9-12

Much love,
Jovie

Also by Jovie

For the most up-to-date printable list of my sweet historical books:

Click here

or go to:

https://www.jografford.com/joviegracebooks

For the most up-to-date printable list of my sweet contemporary books:

Click here

or go to:

https://www.JoGrafford.com/books

About Jovie

Jovie Grace is an Amazon bestselling author of sweet and inspirational historical romance books full of faith, family, and second chances. She also writes sweet contemporary romance as Jo Grafford.

1.) Follow on Amazon!
https://www.amazon.com/author/joviegrace

2.) Join Cuppa Jo Readers!
https://www.facebook.com/groups/CuppaJoReaders

3.) Follow on Bookbub!
https://www.bookbub.com/authors/jovie-grace

4.) Follow on Facebook!
https://www.facebook.com/JovieGraceBooks

Made in United States
North Haven, CT
23 May 2024

52769648R00081